Listening *for* Leroy

BETSY HEARNE

Listening *for* Leroy

MARGARET K. McELDERRY BOOKS

ALSO BY BETSY HEARNE

ELIZA'S DOG

POLAROID AND OTHER POEMS OF VIEW
photographs by Peter Kiar

(MARGARET K. MCELDERRY BOOKS)

Margaret K. McElderry Books
An imprint of Simon & Schuster Children's Publishing Division
1230 Avenue of the Americas
New York, NY 10020

Book design by Michael Nelson

Printed in the United States of America
First Edition
10 9 8 7 6 5 4 3 2

Library of Congress Cataloging-in Publication Data
Hearne, Betsy Gould.
Listening for Leroy / Betsy Hearne.—1st ed.
p. cm.
Summary: Growing up in rural Alabama in the 1950s, eleven-year-old Alice has no one to talk to but Leroy, the black farm hand, but when Alice's doctor father moves the family to Tennessee, she has trouble fitting in and she sorely misses Leroy.
ISBN 0-689-82218-9
[1. Country life—Southern States—Fiction. 2. Family life—Southern States—Fiction. 3. Fathers and daughters—Fiction.
4. Race relations—Fiction. 5. Schools—Fiction. 6. Southern States—Fiction.] I. Title.
PZ7.H3464Li 1998
[Fic]—dc21 98-4495

To Ledford and Johnny Frank, two black men
who brightened my childhood—
to Sam, who had to leave—
and
to my father, who survived the best way
he knew how

Contents

Part I
ALABAMA, 1954-55

Part II
TENNESSEE, 1955-56

Part I
ALABAMA, 1954-55

The Garden

Alice reached her hand slowly toward the snake and touched it with one finger, then jerked back, but the coppery coils wrapped around her wrist like a long muscle, the tail lashing back and forth. She shrieked, shook her arm, and jumped sideways as the snake fell twisting to the ground.

"Get closer, Alice," said her father sharply. "It can't hurt you now."

Maybe it can and maybe it can't, thought Alice.

The snake's head lay to one side where it had fallen when her father chopped it off. Alice stared at the fanged triangle. She tried to crouch closer while her father fiddled with his light meter and finally poised the black box camera.

"Ready, set . . ."

How long could a dead snake keep moving?

"Shoot, I'm out of film. Hold it right there while I run back to the house."

Alice watched her father move away from the beehives,

where the weeds grew tall, along the low garden wall toward the house. In the garden, flowers and vegetables vied for space—red tomatoes with red gladiolas, yellow melons with yellow lilies, purple cabbage with purple phlox, orange carrots underground with orange nasturtiums above, green peas with sweet peas, green beans, green bushes, green leaves everywhere. Bees hummed from the hives her father had started to rob when the copperhead, hidden under some leaves, struck his leather boot.

Alice looked down at her bare feet, half hidden by the dress hanging over her knees. The blue cotton print, sewn from an old flour sack, matched the blue morning glories that twined around the chicken house close by, and matched the silent blue sky above—and also matched her father's blue eyes, watching her even while he was not there. The snake's body twisted and turned more slowly and finally jerked to a stop. Alice's stomach twisted in just the same way.

Did the snake have a mate that might strike in revenge? Did snakes have ghosts? Did snakes' ghosts chase the people who killed them? Would the snake ghost think Alice had killed it because she touched it last and stood beside its dying body? Alice rubbed her hand on the blue dress to get the touch off. Finally her father appeared through the pine trees.

"Stretch out the body, Alice. I want to get a full-length shot. That's a big one."

Wavy patterns circled the snake in shades of light and dark, light and dark, light and dark, all the way to the tapered tail. Except for the blood, it was beautiful, but flies were already arriving. Alice waved them away. The flies were even more disgusting than the snake.

"Be still!" said her father. She froze in the shimmering heat.

"There." Finally, the camera clicked, and clicked, and clicked again, and Alice rose and backed away.

"For pete's sake, Alice, how can you be afraid of a dead snake? You should study that body. Reptiles are a scientific phenomenon of adaptation."

Alice studied her father. He was well over six feet tall, lean, strong, darkly tanned, beautiful and smooth-moving and fearsome, a scientific phenomenon of adaptation.

"If I can finish up this roll of film today, I'll develop the photos after dinner." He lodged his camera in the crook of a tree and picked up the old straw gardening hat that he had covered with mosquito netting for a bee bonnet. As he pulled on a pair of work gloves and approached the hive again, Alice saw the bees swarm around him. Nothing frightened her father. She ran for the barn, the bee-buzz rising faintly behind her like the hiss of a ghost snake. She flashed down the path past poison ivy, past baby chicks that the snake would have swallowed if it could, into the cool, dark barn. Brownie and Patch stopped chewing their hay to stare at her. She stepped between the two cows and leaned her head into their necks, first the honey-brown jersey, just the color of her own hair, and then the huge black-and-white holstein. They smelled sweet and safe.

Slowly, she climbed the ladder into the loft and looked out over the countryside—the fields, the woods, the garden. If she closed her eyes, she could smell each place. The fields smelled of clover; the woods, of long-needle pine trees; and the garden, of ripe tomatoes and rotting melons. The big white house, where her mother was kneading bread dough, smelled of sweet yeast, whole wheat, and honey. The redbrick clinic, where her father tended the sick and injured citizens of Shelby County, smelled of rubbing alcohol. The workers' cottage smelled of steaming laundry, her grandparents' bungalow smelled of mothballs, and the toolshed and chicken coop smelled of dust and must and droppings. Her secret nest in the bamboo grove smelled like fresh-cut grass. The barn below her smelled of Brownie and Patch digesting hay and then splatting the floor with cow pee and poop. There were plenty of smells and sounds, but in all that space not a soul stepped into sight except her father with bees dive-bombing his head. Alice and her father could have been the last two humans on Earth. With the ghost snake circling her mind, she fell asleep in the deep hay.

The sound of Ben clanking buckets woke her, and she listened to the singing of milk on tin as her brother stripped Patch's and Brownie's udders. She lay low while he fed the barn cats and left. Then she heard her mother's call—"Alice! Alice! Alice!"

Once to the East, once to the West, once to the one you love the best. Back up the path, past the chickens, past the poison ivy, past the beehives she ran (not looking at the snake), past the clover, past the pine trees, past the tomatoes and melons, all the way to the back door, slamming the screen.

"Gracious, Alice, you'd wake the dead!" said her mother, leaning down to pull hot bread from the oven. Alice spit over her left shoulder into the sink to keep the dead snake from waking. There were more ways than one to ward off a ghost, and Alice knew them all.

"Look what came in the mail."

On the table was a package, much smaller than her

usual parcel of lesson plans for home-school. Alice opened it slowly. Inside the brown wrapper was a plastic bag of tiny, tight wads of paper.

"The home-schoolers sent spitballs?"

"No, silly, they don't send anything in the summertime. I ordered these for you. Run and get that old fishbowl, Alice, and fill it with cold water."

Before she filled the fishbowl, Alice washed her spit down the drain, and washed her hands carefully with soap. She noticed, for the first time, that the drain looked like a snake hole.

"Now take one of those pellets and drop it in the water."

Alice toted the heavy bowl of water over to the kitchen table and sat down in front of it. Little bubbles of air clouded the water. She picked up a paper spitball and dropped it in. For a minute the spitball floated at the top of the fishbowl. Then it slowly sank toward the bottom, uncurling as if it were alive—a green stem, a leaf, another leaf, a round red flower opening in sudden imitation of spring. Alice's mother sat down across from her and bent sideways to peer through the bowl. They gazed at each other with eyes magnified by the curved glass, two pairs of huge sea-gray eyes staring like fish. Alice dropped another pellet into the water, and they watched it grow, this time into a yellow, bell-shaped blossom. The garden spread across the bottom of the fishbowl, waving in the water as if the wind were blowing her grandmother's prizewinning zinnias.

"It's like the Garden of Eden," whispered Alice, and her breath clouded the glass.

"It might be a little damp for Eden," said her mother.

Alice dropped in another flower, which unfolded bright blue, then an orange and two purple ones.

Alice's mother pushed her chair back. "That's enough, Alice. Save some for another day."

Alice wanted to use them all. She wanted to fill up the fishbowl with floating flowers and dive in and swim through the colors. She looked up and watched her mother move around the steamy kitchen chopping onions, peeling carrots, and kneading ground beef into hamburgers. Snaky tendrils of red meat curled through her fingers. Alice quickly lowered her eyes to the watery Garden of Eden.

"Just one more?"

"No more right now. Set the table while I wash my hands. It's late—your father had a lot of patients waiting for him to finish with the bees. He'll be hungry when he comes home. Here, let me tie your hair back, wild child."

Alice felt her mother's fingers comb her tangled hair into a long braid. Then she felt herself being tugged by the braid, like a dog on a leash, over to a corner drawer.

"Ouch, that pulls," said Alice with her head tilted sideways.

"You don't heel very well," said her mother, searching for a rubber band amidst the buttons and safety pins and paper clips and broken bits and pieces of everything that everyone dumped there.

"There, now you look decent. Go wash your hands."

"I just did." Alice took four plates, four glasses, and four sets of silverware and carefully laid a place at each side of the dining room table. In the center she set the two brass candlesticks, shaped like cobras spreading their hoods, that her father had brought with him from India. The cobras appeared to be weaving in a strange dance to music that no one else could hear . . . or they could be getting ready to strike. Between them she placed a brass vase of gladiolas that her mother had arranged earlier in the day. The spiked flowers separated the cobras like a crimson-and-green screen. Finally she poured the milk, a rich mix from Patch's and Brownie's daily buckets, and tested the pepper grinder to make sure it was full. Her father liked his food spicy.

She was listening to Ben bang his boots on the back porch when her father came up quietly behind her.

"Alice in Wonderland," he whispered.

Alice whirled around. "Daddy, you scared me!"

"Scared? In Wonderland?"

"I'm not Alice in Wonderland. Anyway, she did get scared. Wonderland was awful."

"Worse than setting the table?"

"A lot worse. Setting the table isn't anywhere near as bad."

"Why not?"

"Because."

" 'Because' is not a reason."

"Just because you know it's going to happen. Alice never knew *what* was going to happen."

"Some of her adventures were quite interesting."

"If you like being scared to death."

"Better to die once than a thousand times."

"What does that mean?"

"Being scared all the time is like being in a constant state of death, instead of facing death just once when you have to."

Alice looked at her father. She didn't want to die at all. "Did you develop the snake pictures?" she asked.

"Not yet."

"Will you do it after dinner?"

"We'll see."

Ben padded to his place in bare feet and thumped his big blond handsome self into a chair.

"I set the table, so it's your turn to do the dishes," said Alice.

"I just finished the chores."

"I gathered the eggs this morning while you were galloping around on Lucky Jim."

Her mother came in with steaming dishes in both hands. "Bring in the tomatoes, please, Alice."

Ben made a monkey face at her, and Alice stuck out her tongue at him.

"And the chutney," added her father. "Aren't we about due for a curry dinner?"

Alice's mother looked around the loaded table, her face flushed from cooking in the southern Alabama summer. "Saturday night," she said. Alice's grandparents ate with them Saturday nights. Curry dinners were a lot of work, but Grandmother helped with the chapatis, which she had learned to make in India. Even the thought of chapatis—brown, round, floury, puffy from the hot plate, flattened and rolled around rice and lentils and curried lamb and chutney relish—made Alice happy.

After dinner, her father walked into the living room, past the tall golden harp that her mother played every day, and sat in his leather chair beside the radio. Alice heard static while her father turned the dials from "The Lone Ranger" station to the news. Then a deep, steady, familiar voice said, "Good evening, ladies and gentlemen. Despite the year-old truce, tension continues along the Korean demilitarized zone. . . ."

"Daddy, are you going to—"

"Be quiet," he thundered.

Alice shrank back into the dining room, where Ben was clearing the table.

"You know not to bother him now," said Ben.

Alice retreated through the kitchen toward the back door.

"Stay in the yard, Alice," said her mother. "We'll all go for a walk later on."

Outside the back door an army surplus jeep and a dark red Hudson sat under the carport, crowded close together by a tall pine tree that stuck up through the carport roof on the far side. Alice stepped around the cars and leaned against the pine tree. The pine tree was part of the family because of the biggest fight Alice's parents ever had, which she'd only heard about because it happened before she was born, when they were building the house. The fight was about whether to keep another old pine tree that stood where the living room was supposed to be. Alice's father said to keep the tree and design the living room around it. Alice's mother said that they couldn't have a proper floor and the roof would leak. She won the battle of the living room tree by cutting it down while Alice's father was away on a house call. He was furious and made her promise to keep the tree that stuck up through the carport. They did, and the carport leaked, but nobody cared. It was Alice's favorite pre-Alice story. Her father's pine tree guarded the back of the house like a sentinel.

Her mother had a tree, too, an old mimosa tree with strong gray branches and fragrant flowers like pink powder puffs. Not that her mother ever used pink powder puffs.

She wasn't the type. But her arms seemed like strong branches. Alice wandered over to the mimosa tree, stretched upward, and climbed into the forked limbs that had cradled her body as long as she could remember. Twilight was taking over when she saw a dark figure emerge from the pine woods and move toward her house. She waited till he got right under the tree.

"Hey, Leroy."

"Who's up in that tree?"

"You know who it is, Leroy."

"If this is some kind of ghost, go on home."

Alice slithered down the trunk and dropped to her feet beside Leroy. "Where you going, Leroy?"

"Going to help Myrtle and Zelda get the clinic ready for tomorrow."

"Can I come?"

"Why don't you stay right here and help your mama? She can use all the help she can get."

"Later on, can I?"

"Later on you got to go to bed."

"You got to go to bed, too, Leroy."

"Naw, we don't sleep. We have a party every night after you go to bed."

"You do not. Who all comes?"

"Just our own selves—Myrtle, Zelda, and me."

"You all have a party every night? How come I don't hear any music?"

"We have a real quiet party."

"Just snoring is all. Some party."

Leroy smiled and saluted Alice as he turned down the pine-needled path toward the cottage.

✣ ✣ ✣

They cut their walk short that night. Alice's mother complained of feeling smothered by the heat. She unfolded the old canvas army cot so that Alice could sleep in the screened-in back porch, but there was no cool air anywhere. Their good-night kiss was sticky.

"You won't mind the animals, will you?" asked her mother, bending to release the raccoon and possum from their cages. "They need some exercise. I'll put them away before I go to bed."

Alice lay awake and listened to the skittering of small claws across the linoleum floor. The raccoon was chasing the possum. Orphaned when they were too small for the hunter to stew, both were growing and thriving in her mother's care. A broken-winged owl hooted softly from the perch of its tall, wire cage. Although the owl's call sounded soft, its hooked beak was hard and its eyes were fierce. "Mouse, mouse," glowed the yellow eyes, but the owl had to put up with raw hamburger till its wing healed.

Alice got up to go to the bathroom. As she padded past the tub to the toilet, she heard the hiss of the baby alligator, sharp-toothed, leathery, long-tailed, and abandoned when its owner discovered that birthday presents can bite. Reptile, bird, and mammal—Alice's mother took them all in, like a one-woman animal protection agency. The only animal she hadn't cared for was the garden snake her father kept in the house to catch mice. She found it curled up in her dresser drawer one day and made him take it to the barn. This was another pre-Alice story, not Alice's favorite.

Alice went back to the porch and lay down. Heat seeped through the screens, pressing her against the cot. There was enough wind to sift through the pine tops, but it didn't reach the ground. She rolled over, pushed her hand against the screen, and stared at the pattern of tiny square holes indented on her skin. Alice listened for Leroy singing with his old guitar, but heard no human sound. Mosquitoes whined to get in. A bird called from the trees, *chuck-wills-widow, chuck-wills-widow, chuck-wills-widow.* Something rustled in the bushes outside the screened-in porch. Crickets and cicadas paused in their waves of sound, but the night was too black to see anything except fireflies winking like eerie eyes. What Alice couldn't see was even scarier than what she could.

As if he smelled fear, her father appeared at the door, walked over, and laid his hand on hers.

"Go to sleep," he said.

"I can't. It's too hot."

"It'll cool off by morning. There's a storm coming."

"I wish it would come soon." She wanted thunderclaps and crisp flicks of lightning and the smell of rain mixing up red mud. She wanted the sound of water banging on the roof like a billion tiny hammers. Her father sat on the porch swing and stared into the dark. The coon and possum scuttled under her bed.

"I remember a night like this," he said, "in India when I was a boy at the boarding school. It was just this kind of tense stillness before the monsoons. There was no air in the dormitory, so I took my cotton spread to the outside staircase landing. My parents had told the headmaster to let my brother and me sleep there when the dorm got stuffy. They said it was unhealthy inside, but my brother was afraid to go out. Wild animals used to snoop around at night. And snakes."

Alice pulled the sheet up to her chin. She wanted to hear the story, and she didn't want to hear the story. It helped only a little that she had heard it before.

"Finally I dozed off on the hard floor. In the middle of the night, I woke up. Something was padding up the stairs, some night prowler. It was too heavy for a monkey or mongoose. I pulled the blanket over my head and huddled under it. I had a little penknife that I always carried around my neck and I clutched it for comfort, not that it would have done much good. There was a snuffling sound beside my head, so close, a hot breath. I could feel the thin boards creaking. I thought I was going to die, but I was determined not to give up without a fight."

Alice's father leaned back and fell silent. Alice pulled her sheet tighter.

"The creature nosed my blanket for a long time. Once, I heard a low growl. Then slowly it began to pad away, one step at a time. I lay there, stiff, all night. Before dawn, when the gray light filtered through my blanket, I peered out from under it—first at the floorboards, then along the railing and down the stairs into the jungle. Nothing there. I crept down the stairs, and in the soft earth of the garden below were huge paw prints, a leopard. I could hardly believe I was still alive."

Alice could hardly believe she was still alive herself. She felt as if she'd been holding her breath a long time, from the moment the leopard first padded up the stairs till it padded away across the garden. A garden full of leopard prints. Her father closed her eyes with his long, sun-browned fingers. "Good night," he said softly. The owl hooted again.

"Don't go," she begged, hoping to trick him into reciting some Kipling. Her father could reel off poetry like fishing line.

"What are you scared of?"

"I ain't scared."

"I'm *not* scared. Speak the King's English. You don't need to be afraid," he said. "There's a wire-mesh screen between you and the woods."

But Alice forced her eyes to stay open. Leopards wouldn't have that much trouble with a little wire-mesh screen, and ghost snakes could slither right through it.

The Cottage

No storm came, not even a little rain. Alice woke up to a warm, deep blue dawn. The nocturnal animals were quiet—the owl's eyes closed and its beak tucked into its breast feathers, the possum and coon curled up like furry balls—but the alligator hissed at her in the bathroom, as usual, its mouth wide open and lined with needly teeth. And above the sounds and sleep of saved animals soared the sound of her mother's harp, the first scales for an early morning practice session. She had the metronome going, tock, tock, tock, tock, tock, and her fingers kept perfect time.

da da da da
da da da da da da da
da da da da da da da
da da da da da da Da
Da Da Da dummm

The music of her mother's harp floated from the house to the woods, maybe beyond. Who can say how far a sweet sound reaches? Could her mother be a secret angel? Did angels have to practice scales?

da da da da
da da da da da da da
da da da da da da da
da da da da da da Da
Da Da Da dummm

Alice slipped yesterday's blue dress on, after carefully checking the spot where she had rubbed her hand. There was no trace of snake. She wandered into the kitchen, poured a glass of milk, and slathered peach preserves on the biggest biscuit from the bread box. Then she headed out the back door, dropping crumbs along the way like Hansel and Gretel leaving a trail to find their way home. When she got to the swing, she stopped. She was too old for it, but from the swing she could touch the red rays of the rising sun with the tips of her toes.

The swing sank slightly when she sat down, starting slowly with a stretch of thick ropes and a dip from the branch overhead. She had to push hard against the ground, harder and harder, thudding up dust, skimming toward the treetops with a curve of her body—so high that the swing seemed poised to arc over the branch like a Ferris wheel and turn upside down. She lay back in the whistling air and pointed her feet to sail straight into the new-lit sun.

In the silence of the morning, her mother's daily warning snaked through her thoughts—*You're getting too big for that swing, Alice. It's going to break one of these days.* Alice slowed down, pulled her toes from the sun to the earth, and dragged her heels through two grooves worn in the dirt. The leathery bottoms of her bare feet scraped to a stop as she sat and wondered what to do next.

Suddenly the swing was pulled backward, and she was airborne again. Smooth, strong strokes lifted her into flight. Alice closed her eyes. "Daddy?" There was no answer except the boost from behind, over and over and over. Then it stopped, and her father left without a word. She floated down, rocking to a stop in the still air. The joy that had filled her flattened. Alice sat twirling the swing back and forth, twisting it around and around, missing something. Now it was lonely, swinging alone. She wished her father would come back and push her in the swing all morning instead of going to work at the clinic. She wished her mother would call her into the house to make another water garden. She wished her brother would play with her like he used to. Three wishes. But the summer sat still.

Alice saw the back door open and watched Ben leave the house, heading for the barn to saddle Lucky Jim. *Ride a white horse to Banbury Cross/ To see a fine lady upon a cock-horse.* Except Lucky Jim was brown and Alice didn't ride him. From far away he was beautiful, but up close he was tall and skittery. Alice wanted something closer to the ground. Something not wild. A dog, for instance—she would settle for the company of a dog. Barn kittens were wild by the time they were weaned. Cows were lovable, but they resisted house-training. Coons and possums and alligators and owls went back to the woods sooner or later. Chickens got eaten. Alice was not friendly with chickens, even though egg collecting was her responsibility.

She ran back to the porch, picked up a basket, and went down the path toward the chicken coop. Near the garden, her eyes wandered sideways from the path. The snake looked smaller, already starting to mix with the earth. Flies were busy with the head. Ants were turning the body into a long, thin cage of bones. Alice forced her attention straight ahead and stooped to enter the chicken coop, setting her basket on the floor.

The coop was a shack with built-in shelves along the

inside walls, where the chickens could nest. It was dark inside and draped with dusty spiderwebs. Droppings crackled and smeared underfoot. She had to thrust her hand into the straw under the chickens, which clucked fiercely, shook their combs, and stared with beady eyes. Mean Minnie beat her wings in Alice's face and pecked her hand. Alice waved her arms, screeching, "SHOO SHOO SHOO." When Mean Minnie rose up on her scaly yellow legs, Alice grabbed an egg and backed away to add it to her basket.

"Half a cent, plus half a cent, plus half a cent, plus half a cent . . . ," whispered Alice to the chickens. "Ten eggs is five cents." Five cents bought two chocolate almonds. It would take dozens of chocolate almonds to fill up the heart-shaped box she'd made for her mother's Christmas present. That's why she had to start so far ahead. The chocolate almonds were small, and the box was large, but she had months to work on it.

Alice wiped her feet clean on some dewy grass and carried the basket back up the path, past the garden and house. She zigzagged among towering pine trees and skirted the bamboo grove where she kept her own secret nest, larger than the chickens' but small enough to hide in. She paused alongside the swimming pool her father had dug with a tractor and lined with concrete. The water reflected the aqua paint of the pool walls. Alice looked longingly at it, but she couldn't go in unless an adult was around. Her father had set up a spiked fence to make sure of that.

Near the white wooden cottage that served as kitchen and laundry for the clinic, she could hear Myrtle and Zelda laughing with Leroy. She ducked through some fragrant crepe myrtle bushes, peered around the flypaper on the screen door, and knocked on the wooden frame.

"Well, look who's here—a big fine girl, just what we need," called Zelda. "And some eggs, which we also need. And the good Lord knows I need a break! Come churn this butter for a while, honey."

Alice piled her eggs into a huge blue crockery bowl on the table and slid along a bench toward Zelda. They bumped hips beside the wooden barrel. Then Zelda let go of the crank, and Alice began to turn it around and around as the wooden paddle gathered butter on its blades and left thick buttermilk in its wake. Sweat slid down her neck.

"It's hot in here, Zelda."

"Hot because you're working."

"Look at those muscles," said Leroy.

"She could stand to plump up some," said Myrtle. Her round brown arms shone in the sunlight slanting through the window.

"You know, I never thought about this before, Myrtle," said Alice, "but you know those crepe myrtle bushes? Did they name you after those flowers?"

"Yes, they did!" said Leroy. "That's what they did, all right. Just call her Crepe."

"Watch out, Leroy, or I'll call you what you are," said Myrtle.

"So sweet, so sweet the smell of Myrtle!"

"Shut up, Leroy, that's enough out of you," said Zelda. "Leave my sister alone or I'll give you what for."

"What for?" asked Leroy.

"You know what for, being your own bad self."

"Leroy's not bad," said Alice.

"No, he just pretends all the time," said Myrtle.

"Is this butter ever going to get done?" asked Alice.

"It's just about done, sugar. Go on now and say hey to your grandmama. She's trying to get ready for the Missionary Circle potluck."

"I could use some of that kind of luck," said Leroy.

"Hunh, those ladies don't want to feed the likes of you," snapped Zelda.

"Maybe they do and maybe they don't," said Leroy, smiling slyly at Zelda. "How would you know, honey?"

Alice waited for Zelda to tell Leroy to shut up again because she loved hearing it, but instead Zelda flipped her hand, meaning *upside your head*. If Zelda had been closer, she might have hit Leroy upside the head, which she did when Leroy got too fresh. Alice wanted to try it out on Ben, but she didn't dare because he would pulverize her. When Zelda hit Leroy upside the head, he just ducked and had a laughing attack.

Zelda bumped hips with Alice again and shoved her over on the bench.

"Go on, now, before big bad Leroy starts moving his mouth again."

"Bye, honey, come again," said Myrtle.

Before Alice got out the door, she heard Zelda reply, "Reckon she'll come with the eggs tomorrow morning, like she always does. That Alice, she's a big fine girl."

"She could stand to plump up some," said Myrtle.

Down the pathway through the dark pines stood her grandparents' brown bungalow. *Bungalow* was a word from the Hindi language, which Grandmother spoke with Alice's father when she didn't want Alice to know what they were saying. *Bungalow* was what Grandmother called her house in India, and *bungalow* was what she called her house in Alabama. Grandmother did not change much, wherever she lived, thought Alice. Why didn't she just say *house*? Or *cottage* would be nice. That's what a bungalow really was, a cottage. There was the white cottage, where Myrtle and Zelda worked, with Leroy teasing them, and there was the brown cottage, where Grandmother always got her way—so *bungalow* it was, a gingerbread house waiting for her behind the trees. "A brown *cottage*," muttered Alice to herself.

From here, Alice could see her grandmother's zinnias flashing like the colors in a kaleidoscope, and she could hear Pixie barking frantically. Alice's dog was not going to be a prissy little terrier that yapped all the time, like Pixie. Grandmother opened the door looking hot and flustered. Three hairpins hung halfway out of the bun on the back of her head.

"Come, Pixie! Come in, Alice. You're just in time. I need some help with the fruit salad."

Alice walked carefully around the rug, made from the skin of a leopard that Grandfather had shot in his backyard in India before retiring from the mission field. That was the story Grandmother told, anyway. Grandfather never said anything. The leopard's fur was golden-brown with black spots. Daddy said it was not the same leopard that padded up the boardinghouse stairs, but how did he know? All he saw were the footprints. Alice thought it was the same leopard. Even though its four legs stretched flat on the floor, its head was stuffed to rise up round and real, yellow eyes glowing, long teeth bared in a snarl that was larger by far than snake fangs. Pixie stepped around it, too.

Alice held her breath all the way through the living room, where Grandfather puffed on his stinky cigar. Through rings of smoke he stared at a row of tiny elephants, carved from ebony and ivory, that stood trumpeting on the teak table. Grandfather's mind lived far away.

"Hurry, Alice, there's so much to do. I want you to peel these apples and slice them and don't eat any. We have just enough. Call me when you're finished, and we'll add walnuts and celery and raisins and mayonnaise. I have to finish cleaning the bathroom. And I'm putting you on your honor not to eat those apples, young lady. Just remember, even if I don't see everything you do, there is One Above who does."

Alice stood at the sink. The bowl of apples looked like a red mountain. She began paring—paring and paring and paring—staring at the thick, succulent red peels curling away from her knife. The breakfast biscuit was long gone. Grandmother had not forbidden her to eat peels. The tough, sweet skins tasted like tutti-frutti chewing gum. As she munched and sliced, munched and sliced, each peel got thicker and thicker. With so much munching in her ears, she did not hear Grandmother appear at the door.

"Alice!"

"Yes, ma'am?"

"What are you doing?"

"Peeling the apples."

"Young lady, I told you not to eat any apples."

"I'm not eating the apples," cried Alice. "I'm eating the peels."

"What you are doing is stretching the truth. Stretching the truth is just as bad as lying."

Grandmother looked at Alice reproachfully, clasped her arm, and pulled her into a dining room chair. "You've betrayed my trust. Go upstairs by yourself and think about the difference between truth and lies. God hates a liar. He sees into your heart, and He knows the truth. The next time you want to twist the truth in word or deed, you think about that. Think about what happens to everyone who disobeys Him."

Alice clumped slowly up the stairs. She knew what happened to everyone who disobeyed Him. They went to Hell. That's what Grandmother and the preacher said, anyway. And the air upstairs felt like Hell, even though Heaven was supposed to be up and Hell was supposed to be down. In Alabama, Heaven and Hell must be reversed, because the cellar was always cool, cool and safe. That's where they went during tornadoes. Alice yearned to be in the cellar of her own house right now, eating apples. That's what got Eve into trouble in the Garden of Eden, eating an apple, eating the fruit of knowledge, listening to the serpent. It didn't seem fair. Why shouldn't Eve eat the apple and why shouldn't God want her to have knowledge and why was there an evil serpent in a garden that was supposed to be perfect? And why shouldn't Alice eat apple skins and why did God make snakes dangerous, anyway? None of it was fair. God was not fair.

She tried to open the windows, but they were all stuck. With the windows closed, the heat in the attic bedroom soared above a hundred degrees. Even so, the attic was probably not as hot as Hell. On the hottest, hottest Sunday noons, the preacher glared at the paper fans waving in the pews before him and yelled, "The heat in Alabama does not compare with the heat in Hell—and Hell, Brothers and Sisters, is a hot place to spend forever."

Liars roasted in Hell. As she closed her eyes and imagined red flames peeling her body, Alice heard a low, buzzing sound. She opened her eyes. Up in the corner under the roof was a tiny dark hole that appeared to serve as a doorway for wasps. They were clumped in a writhing knot of wings, legs, and feelers. Alice watched them, hypnotized. Like a bad dream, several of them peeled off from the cluster and flew around her. She batted at them and turned to run through the door, but they circled around her head like a ghost snake. One or two landed close to the bridge of her nose. A burning pain shot through her face. She yelled and stumbled down the stairs, slamming the door behind her.

Grandmother appeared at Alice's side as if by magic. Without a word, she wrapped ice in a dish towel and pressed it against Alice's face, swollen and wet with tears. The ghost snake had gotten even. Rest in peace. Walking toward the door, they skirted the leopard-skin rug and pools of cigar smoke. The smoke smelled terrible. The smoke was a leopard ghost, stealing Grandfather's mind to get even for being made into a rug.

"Keep that ice on till you get home, Alice."

Alice felt cold water melt between her fingers as she pressed the ice pack to her face and looked up at her grandmother's wrinkled forehead. She couldn't tell, from the deep frown, whether Grandmother was worried or angry.

"Are you going to tell them?" she asked, her voice choked small from crying.

"Tell them what?"

"That I lied about the apples."

"No, my dear," said Grandmother softly. "You have been punished enough."

So Alice would not go to Hell for this sin. But if God and Grandmother and the preacher were all in Heaven together, Alice was not sure she wanted to go there, either.

The Cabin

"Alice, are you going with Daddy on house calls?"

"Hunh-unh. I look too funny with my face all puffed up."

"Don't say 'hunh-unh.' Say 'no, ma'am.' And nobody cares how you look."

"I do."

"Alice, I want you to get out of this house. You've been brooding for days."

"Oh, Mother."

"Go on, now, Alice, and no back talk." Only once had Alice back talked, a long time ago. She'd heard a friend of Ben's say *shut up* and tried it out on her mother, who washed her mouth out with soap. Even thinking *shut up* made Alice's mouth taste slimy. Slowly she walked toward the clinic, where she spied her father standing by the gardenia bush. The gardenia bush was like a statue of Heaven and Hell. Its flat, white, waxy flowers filled the air with perfume. Then they fell and rotted in little brown heaps.

"Hi, pie-face."

"Daddy! Don't make fun of me."

"I won't if you'll keep me company. We've got to take the jeep. Leroy's mother is sick, and that road is pure rock."

"She was sick last week."

"Leroy's mother may not get well, Alice."

"Poor Leroy."

"Leroy takes good care of her."

Alice and her father climbed into the jeep and headed toward the backwoods road. Branches and bushes whipped the canvas that was snapped around the jeep's iron ribs. Sharp stones jarred the wheels, and mud sucked on the tires. Alice's father shifted into four-wheel drive.

"When are you going to teach me how to drive, Daddy?"

"One of these days. It's Ben's turn right now."

"I could start on the tractor."

"That's a rough ride."

"I can do it. Ben drove the tractor when he was my age."

"Ben was a lot bigger than you are."

"But you always say I'm growing like a weed!" protested Alice.

"You're tall and thin, Alice. Ben is heavier and stronger. He can handle a stiff steering wheel and gearshifts."

"Well, it's not fair. You ought to at least let me try."

"Okay, we can try you out on the tractor."

"By myself?"

"Not to start with."

One side of the road tilted upward toward a hill covered with kudzu vines. The jeep slanted sideways as if it would turn over, and then righted itself with a bounce. Alice grabbed the roll bar and hung on.

"What's that tree, Alice?"

"Cedar."

"How about the sapling there?"

"Sassafras."

"Okay, name the next three you see."

"Long-needle pine, ailanthus, and willow."

"Too easy. You need a new stretch of woods."

"Leroy and his mama sure live far back."

"Nobody bothers them back here."

"Who would bother them, anyway?"

"The same people who were standing around when Leroy's father got killed in an accident at the sawmill."

"What kind of accident?"

"An accident on purpose, I suspect."

"You mean he got murdered?"

"There's no proof, and it was a long time ago, but Leroy's just like his father. He's smart, and he speaks his mind. That doesn't win you any popularity contests around here."

"You're smart, and you speak your mind."

"I'm white, Alice. And I'm the only doctor for forty-five miles around."

They pulled up to the cabin, and Alice's father reached for his brown bag that smelled of leather and medicine and opened up into two trays of instruments, with bottles and cotton and bandages and tape underneath. He could deliver a baby with his bag, or splint a broken leg, or do surgery, or drag a person out from under an overturned burning tractor and save his life. He had done all those things. He was famous for them.

"Come on in, Alice. Louise would like to see you."

An old hound barked at them as Alice hauled herself out of the jeep and followed her father. Leroy's house was divided in half by a long, open hallway that stretched from the front porch to the back—a shotgun cabin. Somebody could shoot a shotgun from front to back without hitting anything, unless he wanted to hit something. Alice stayed close behind her father. The kitchen and parlor were on one side, two bedrooms on the other. An old wood-burning stove heated the kitchen and parlor in wintertime, but its black iron was cold now.

As if she felt the cold of the stove through the heat of the day, Leroy's mother huddled under a patchwork quilt in the parlor rocking chair. She was not much older than Alice's mother, but the sharp bones of her face and hands stretched her skin tight. Alice's father put down his bag and took out the stethoscope.

"Hello, Louise. How do you feel?"

"So-so, Doc Ryder. Alice, how you've grown! But what's wrong with your face, honey? You're all swollen up."

"Just some wasp stings, is all. They don't hurt anymore."

"Looks like you knocked down the whole nest with your nose! We used to daub mud on wasp stings when I was little. Funniest thing you ever saw was one of us kids running around looking like a mud-head." Suddenly Leroy's mother scrunched her face up and caught her breath. She held it for a minute and then let it out slowly, as if breathing hurt her stomach. Then she opened her eyes again. "Aren't you sweet to come along with your Daddy, Alice. There's a plate of peaches in the kitchen, honey—go pick one out for yourself, a nice big juicy one."

Alice turned into the kitchen, took a soft ripe peach, and went out to sit on the porch. Above the murmur of voices, she could hear woods noise, the tiny mysterious snapping sounds that might be beetles chewing or pinecones dropping or rodents scuttling through the underbrush. She thought about Leroy's daddy not coming home one day, or the next, or the next, and Leroy and his mama listening to the woods noise and not hearing his voice again. The hound flopped down beside Alice. He smelled of swamp water with a little skunk thrown in. She held out her hand for him to sniff and rubbed his long, soft ears. Here and there was a hard lump of scar tissue where he'd been hurt, bitten maybe. Could be raccoon bites. A big raccoon would fight back if it was cornered. Just about anything would fight back if it was cornered. Even the barn cats got mean. Alice had scratch scars from trying to pick up kittens that looked cute but didn't like to be cornered.

After a while, her father appeared and motioned her into the jeep.

"Should I say good-bye?"

"Louise is almost asleep now, Alice. I gave her some pain pills and put her to bed. She had a bad night."

"What's wrong with her, Daddy?"

"She has cancer."

"Shouldn't she come to the clinic?"

"There's not much more we can do for her now except make her comfortable. Leroy took her to a hospital in Birmingham, but she'd rather be home now."

Alice ducked as a branch slapped the windshield.

"You can't duck if you're going to drive," said her

father. "You've got to keep your eyes on the road."

"I will. I promise I will, Daddy, no matter what."

"When we get our Cadillac and live in a twenty-room mansion on the Gulf of Mexico, it'll be easier."

Alice laughed. "When will that be?"

"As soon as my ship comes in. You can have a yachting party for all your friends."

"Daddy, I don't have any friends. We live too far away from everybody. And we won't be rich as long as your patients pay you with chickens and beans."

"You never know. I just might strike gold one of these days."

Alice thought of her mother's harp. They had gold.

"What would you buy first?" asked her father.

"What would I buy first?"

"If I struck gold, what would you buy?"

"A dog."

"It doesn't take a lot of money to get a dog."

"Well, that's what I want."

"Don't we already have enough animals to populate the ark?"

"All I want is a dog."

"We'll have to see about that. Your mother has too much to take care of already."

"I'll take care of it."

"You take care of the dog, I'll take care of the mansion. Right now, I'd better take care of the road." Alice's father concentrated on keeping the jeep upright and unstuck from the dried-mud ruts. When they got back home, he called Ben from the barn. "Let's take the jeep out in the field, son, you need some practice."

"Can I come, too?" asked Alice.

"If you hang on tight."

Alice climbed into the back of the jeep and sat on one of the metal benches that lined each side. The benches opened up to hold tools and chains that rattled with every bump. The noise was louder in the back, and the bouncing was harder. Alice's father settled on the front passenger seat as Ben climbed in the driver's side. Ben pushed his feet down on the clutch and brake, started the engine, and shifted from neutral into first gear. Then he sat for a moment, gripping the steering wheel so hard, his knuckles turned white.

"Well, son, if we're going anywhere you have to take your foot off the brake."

Ben quickly lifted his right foot.

"And the clutch."

Ben let up on the clutch with his left foot and pressed his right foot on the gas pedal. The jeep plunged forward like a charging bull and then died, sending Alice crashing sideways into the back of her father's seat.

"Alice, I told you to hang on," said her father over his shoulder. Alice curled a hand around the roll bar and squeezed to the beat of the throbbing pain in her ribs.

"Now, son, think about driving the tractor. You have to let up on the clutch and give it just enough gas at the same time. And don't forget to use the brake if you need to."

Sweat streaked Ben's blond hair and ran down his neck. He banged on the steering wheel with both hands. "It feels different from the tractor."

"Of course it's different from the tractor. You have to get used to it."

This time the jeep lurched to life but did not stop, and they careened down the gravel driveway toward the red-dirt county road. Pebbles and dust spurted up behind them.

"Cross the road and head for the fields," shouted Alice's father. "You're not ready for the road yet."

The jeep stopped just short of smashing into the gate, which Alice's father unlatched and then latched again after Ben drove through. Brownie and Patch looked up suspiciously from the corner of the field where they had been grazing in peace all morning, and Lucky Jim cantered uneasily along the fence.

"Okay, take it away," said Alice's father. Ben roared headlong across clover, grass, rocks, and cow paddies, some old and dry, some new and squashy. The jeep veered wildly back and forth. Alice's backside left the bench and reconnected with bone-cracking thumps as metal clanked back and forth in the storage space beneath her.

"You don't have to turn the steering wheel so hard, Ben. It's not as stiff as the tractor."

Ben's face twisted in concentration. Brownie and Patch watched the jeep crashing toward them, bellowed madly, stuck their tails straight up in the air, and stampeded. Ben whirled the wheel away from them.

"Slow down, son! And remember, if it's a choice between hitting an animal or swerving to avoid it and maybe hitting another car with people in it, stay on your own side of the road." Alice closed her eyes. She had been in the car when her father made this choice, and there was not always another car coming. Not one she could see, anyway. You never knew what was coming around the corner, but what if the road was straight? What if you could see way down the road? Did you have to kill a little animal in order to obey the rule? Wasn't that just pure cruelty? Even the sight of roadkills made her sick.

"Well, a *cow*, Daddy," she shouted. "You have to stop for a cow. A cow could wreck the car."

"If you see a cow coming, Alice, pull slowly to a stop. On your own side of the road."

Ben drove the jeep around the field in a large circle, careful to leave a wide space between the jeep and Lucky Jim, Brownie, and Patch—all backed nervously into a stand of trees. Gradually Ben's fists unclenched into fingers around the steering wheel. He leaned back slightly and seemed to breathe again. Twice he stopped and started the jeep with barely a jolt.

"That's about enough for today, Ben. Let's get on home."

"But I'm just getting started."

"Starting is the hard part."

"But . . ."

"No arguments."

Ben clamped his mouth shut. Alice could see his jaw muscles twitch and she knew that he was still arguing even if he didn't say it out loud.

As the jeep wobbled back across the field, they saw Leroy beside the fence with a smile gleaming across his face. His skin was almost blue-black in the sun, and muscles stood out on his arms as he unlatched and pulled the gate open. Anybody would be crazy to mess with Leroy, thought Alice. His cabin in the woods was safe.

Leroy saluted her father. "Looks like you got yourself a chauffeur, Doc."

"Just give us plenty of room," said Alice's father.

Leroy pulled the gate all the way back while the jeep jerked its way forward across the road and up the driveway into the carport, stopping an inch away from the pine tree. With a final roar, the engine died, and an immense stillness descended. Alice's body felt like a collection of stones rattled around in her father's rock-polishing machine. She climbed stiffly out of the jeep.

"Ben, take Alice on down to the barn and show her how to work the gears on the tractor." Ben scowled at her but dared not say anything, since he had just gotten a lesson himself.

Alice yearned to go into the kitchen for a drink of water, retreat into her bamboo nest with a book, and read the rest of the day. Her face still felt feverish from wasp stings, or maybe it was the heat of the blazing sun in the open field. She stood poised on the steps of the porch.

"You coming?" asked Ben.

Her father watched her with a dare-you look in his deep blue eyes. If she turned this offer down, there wouldn't be another one soon. Anybody who drove a tractor had to be tough enough to stand a little bouncing around.

Alice sighed. "I'm coming," she said. Her father gave a satisfied smile and stepped into the kitchen.

The Pool

"Daddy, can we go in the pool this morning?" asked Alice. "It's so hot." The morning sun was already melting the air into shimmering waves. Alice's mother was organizing peppery spices in the kitchen.

"I've got surgery this morning, Alice, and house calls."

"But it's Saturday!"

"Emergencies don't wait for office hours."

Alice sighed and looked at her mother through the open doorway. No use. Her mother never had learned to swim because she said it was too cold up north where she grew up. She wouldn't even go in the water without a black rubber inner tube to keep her afloat.

"Don't worry," said her father. "We'll go in this afternoon. It'll be even hotter then."

"I want to go now," grumbled Alice.

"What did you say?" asked her father sharply.

"Nothing."

"It didn't sound like nothing to me. It sounded like sulking."

"I'm sorry, Daddy, but there's nothing to do."

"You could go see your grandmother."

Alice was silent.

"What did you say?"

"She's coming here tonight, Daddy," said Alice hastily.

"What about your work?"

"I already gathered the eggs, and the dishes don't take long, and I don't have to study in summertime."

"Why don't you play with Ben?"

Ben glared across the table at their father. "I'm fourteen," he reminded his father sharply, "and I'm going riding just like I always do."

"Fourteen is old enough to save your sister from drowning. Here's the padlock key for the pool gate. You're in charge."

Alice watched Ben cloud, brighten, and cloud again. She could translate his face—mad to be stuck with her but proud to be grown up but not sure which to be more of, mad or proud.

"Does this mean Pete and Chuck can swim, too?"

"Not until you've proved yourself capable of lifeguarding Alice for a while. I'm not ready for a community lawsuit."

Ben drained his glass of milk and stood up to his full height, which Alice saw was inching toward his father's.

"All right, come on, baby sister."

Alice's father shoved back from the table and looked Ben full in the eyes, blue against blue. "A little more respect all around," he commanded quietly. "And you've forgotten the cardinal rule: Wait a half hour after eating. I don't want to hear about stomach cramps."

Ben swallowed nervously. "We'll go muck out the horse stall first."

Alice trotted behind him toward the barn. "You're walking too fast, Ben."

"Keep up, then."

"You're being mean. Just because I'm younger than you are and don't get to go to school doesn't mean I'm a baby."

"You act like a baby."

"You act like a big shot. You didn't used to be like this. You used to do stuff with me."

"Like what?"

"You know, like camping out."

"In the backyard," said Ben scornfully.

"And playing pirates on the raft."

"Big deal."

"Just because your friends are mean doesn't mean you have to be mean. You just want to show how tough you are. I don't care. I liked you better before."

Ben didn't reply, but he handed her a brush from the barn wall and showed her how to start currying Lucky Jim while he shoveled out the dirty straw underfoot. Lucky Jim reached back and nuzzled Alice in the neck and tossed his head at Ben.

"He's beautiful, Ben. I wish I could ride him."

"Lucky Jim is mine!"

"I know that, stupid," yelled Alice. She hid behind Lucky Jim's barrel-round belly. "Nobody's going to take your stupid horse away from you." Alice brushed blindly along the sleek swirls of Lucky Jim's brown rump.

"Okay, okay," mumbled Ben. He did not say that only babies cried.

When the stall was clean and Lucky Jim was gleaming, with hay in the manger and fresh water in the trough, Ben grabbed the bucket, threw the rest of the water over Alice's head, and yelled, "Race you to the pool!"

Alice ducked around him and flew out the door, up the path, past the beehives and rotting snake, and around the back of the house. Ben lumbered behind her, his sturdy legs hampered in rubber boots. The water of the pool gleamed blue-green behind the diamond pattern of the high spiked fence, which Alice crashed into with both arms shielding her face.

"Beat you," she shouted.

"Because you had sneakers on," panted Ben, crashing next to her. Sweat poured down his face as the fence pinged back and forth from the force of their impact.

"Ha-ha," taunted Alice, "so you say." But she smiled at him, and he punched her arm in a friendly way. Then he pulled the key from his pocket.

"Don't forget who's in charge," he said with a grand flourish.

"Don't drop the key behind the fence."

Ben inserted the key, the padlock sprang open, and they pulled back the gate. Alice darted behind the bushes at one corner of the pool and changed into the bathing suit she'd hung on a branch to dry the day before. Then she ran to the edge of the pool while Ben changed.

"Don't go in yet!" he called through the leaves.

"Don't forget to take your boots off!" she called back.

Ben charged out of the bushes and dove into the pool before she could say anything else. She cannonballed after him and landed in a round ball that spurted a volcano of water into the air. They fought to climb onto the tiny raft.

Ben won, tipping the whole thing toward him and throwing himself stomach first onto the smooth wooden boards.

"I am the captain and you are the victim," he crowed, standing tipsily on the raft. "You have just walked the plank and will die forthwith."

"Not I!" Alice screamed, and she grabbed the other side and pushed it down so that Ben had to dive or fall off.

He churned toward her.

"No ducking!" shrieked Alice as she lunged her body away from him.

"Sorry, your face looks like a beach ball," panted Ben.

Alice stuck her head underwater. The swelling in her cheeks and forehead was going down. She did not look like a beach ball.

The pool was bath-warm, but the air drying on her skin above the surface of the water cooled her off. When she and Ben tried to climb out, the concrete pavement burned, so they stayed in the water till their fingers and toes wrinkled. Together they swam laps, dove to the bottom, and floated flat on the surface, closing their eyes against the molten sun. Little black bugs and shadowy water spiders skimmed the water beside them. Alice seemed part of the water itself, gently rocking in the waves.

Suddenly she felt a bite on her backside and screeched to a tread-water position.

"Mother let the alligator loose," sputtered Ben, his eyes red from swimming underwater. "It's coming after you."

"She did not. That was you."

Ben grinned and dove again. Alice swam as fast as she could to the side of the pool and heaved herself up just as

Ben grabbed her foot and pulled her back down. Alice slipped away from him, circled, dove, and pinched his thrashing legs.

When her head popped up from the water like a seal, she heard a deep voice from the fence. "Don't drown your brother."

"Daddy, come on in!"

"I'm on my way out. I just wanted to check on you two. Good job, Ben. You can go ride your horse now."

Ben turned redder than his sunburn and ducked his head in the water. Alice pleaded.

"Not yet, come on, Ben. We just got in."

"We've been here for hours. It's after noon."

"Please, please, just a little bit longer."

"Stop whining, Alice. I gotta go meet Chuck." Ben backstroked to the end of the pool and climbed onto the pavement, run-hopping behind the bushes to dry off and change. Alice waited in the water for her turn. After they had spread their suits over the top of the bushes for the next swim, Ben carefully locked the gate behind them, pocketed the key, and marched off toward the barn in his rubber boots.

"Thanks, Ben," called Alice.

Ben gave her a backhanded wave, and Alice wandered toward the mimosa tree to watch him ride off into the woods on Lucky Jim.

"Yoo-hoo," called Alice's grandmother at the door.

Alice and her mother looked at each other across the mess in the kitchen. "Go help your grandmother, Alice. I'll finish up here."

Alice passed through the kitchen door and dining room into the living room. Nobody in the world said *Yoo-hoo* except in Li'l Abner cartoons.

"Hi, Grandmother."

"Good evening, Alice. Have you recovered from your battle with the wasps?"

"Yes, thank you. I'm feeling much better."

"You're looking much better, too, just some slight swelling here and there. Could you take this apple salad to your mother, please, so I can help Sinclair take a chair?"

Help *Sinclair* take a *chair*? Alice tried to keep her slightly swollen face from cracking into a rude smirk. Her grandmother handed over the bowl and led her grandfather toward the large easy chair beside the radio.

"That's Daddy's chair," said Alice automatically.

"I'm sure your father won't mind giving up his chair to his own father for one evening, Alice."

Alice looked down at the chopped apples and celery and walnuts and raisins piled in their sweet mayonnaise dressing. Why did she always say the wrong thing to Grandmother?

"Go help your mother, now, Alice, while I settle Sinclair. I'll be in directly to start the chapatis."

At that moment, Alice's father walked into the living room.

"Hello, Father. Hello, Mother," he said formally.

Alice's grandmother nodded to him but her grandfather gazed sternly into the air as if he were listening to voices from above. *Senile dementia*, Alice's father called it, Latin for old-age insanity. Grandfather seemed not to recognize where he was or who he was with or what day it was. His eyes were open while his mind was asleep. Stolen by the leopard ghost. Alice's grandmother switched on the radio to keep him company and went into the kitchen.

After a last-minute rush of setting the table and spooning food from cooking pots to china dishes and resettling Alice's grandfather into yet another chair, they all gathered at the table. Bowls of rice and curried lamb and lentils steamed from hand to hand. Silver spoons dipped into mango chutney and cold yogurt. Alice took a polite portion of apple salad. An electric hot plate beside Alice's grandmother burned fiery red as she slapped on flat rounds of whole wheat dough to grill and puff up. It was hard to wait for the first chapati. Alice forked a mixture of curry, rice, and chutney onto the chapati and then rolled it up, taking a huge bite out of the end and dripping bits and pieces on her plate.

"Aren't we forgetting something?" asked Alice's grandmother. Alice's mother dropped her head and closed her eyes, as did everyone else at the table.

"For this food we thank thee, O Lord, and for keeping us all safe together, amen."

"Amen," said Alice's grandfather in a loud voice.

Everyone stared at him in surprise, but he was studying his plate as if it were scripture and did not look up.

"Well, that was short and sweet," said Alice's father, "so let's eat!" He took a chapati and, without dropping a grain of rice—without using knife, fork, or spoon—scooped up a neat bite.

"Look at all this food. Whenever I think of those we left behind in India . . . ," sighed Alice's grandmother, transferring another chapati from the hot plate to the pile in the woven basket. "So much hunger, so much injustice."

"There's plenty of hunger and injustice right here at home," said Alice's mother.

"Not like there, Lydia. You just can't imagine."

"I can look around me, though."

"It's not the same. Think of a caste system that labels people Untouchables."

"We have one just like it here," said Alice's mother stubbornly. "Segregation is a caste system. One group with power discriminates against another group without power. It's that simple."

Alice's grandmother sighed again. "We pray for those in Alabama, too."

"It's going to take more than praying," said Alice's father.

Alice watched Ben twist his napkin. He had shoveled down all his food, and Alice knew he wanted to go night-fishing at the creek with Chuck and Pete. She also knew that what her parents were saying made Ben nervous. Chuck and Pete teased him about having a Yankee mother and an Indian father even though Ben explained over and over that his father was born in India but was really American. Personally, Alice couldn't see what difference it made. What did it matter whether their father was Indian or American, anyway? But it mattered to Ben, because it mattered to his friends. Alice had overheard them arguing in Ben's room one day. Ben's friends didn't come to the house often. Nobody did. People could forgive Alice's father being from India, because everybody in town needed a doctor and besides, his parents were missionaries. But Alice's mother was from Michigan, and being a Yankee was sinful. It was worse than being a foreigner.

While Ben fidgeted, Alice watched the faces around

the table bead with sweat, especially her father's as he nibbled on pickled peppers so hot that Alice couldn't even taste one without burning her tongue. She gulped down iced tea in sympathy and turned her face to catch a breath of breeze whirring from the electric fan in the corner. Despite the French doors that her mother had propped open as far as possible, the dining room felt like a campfire.

On the floury brown surface of her last chapati, Alice spread melting butter and brown sugar. Then she rolled it up like a cigar and took a huge bite.

"Good gracious, Alice, you needn't eat like a savage beast," said her grandmother. Ben snickered and kicked her under the table. Her parents looked at each other but didn't say a word, and her grandfather stared out the window as Alice took another bite.

"Can I be excused?" asked Ben.

"After you help your sister with the dishes," said Alice's mother.

Alice grinned at him and chewed the end of her dripping chapati like a savage beast.

The Pasture

Alice stared at the photographs on the living room mantelpiece. On one side of the hinged gold frame was a picture of Ben riding Lucky Jim, and on the other side, a picture of Ben smiling into the camera with a huge bull snake twisting around his neck. Ben was holding the snake like a feather boa. Why wasn't Alice as brave as Ben?

"Daddy? What happened to the picture you took of me and the copperhead?"

"It didn't turn out, Alice." He snapped open the cover of *Life* magazine.

"What was wrong with it?"

"The film was overexposed. You looked like a ghost."

"Oh. . . . Daddy?"

"What?"

"Can you teach me how to ride Lucky Jim?"

"He's pretty wild, Alice. Just take one thing at a time— you'll have your hands full with the tractor. Ben says you can't even manage the gear shifts yet." That was true. Alice had to use both hands for the gear shifts, and you were supposed to keep one hand on the steering wheel, plus the clutch was too far to reach and hard to jam down. But Ben didn't have to tell on her. And a horse didn't have a clutch and gearshift. On the other hand, a horse could run away with you. Stupid Ben would never let her ride Lucky Jim, anyway.

Alice tried to concentrate on her math lesson. A new packet of home-school materials for fall had just arrived, and her mother wanted her to start reviewing them even though it was only August. Why should she have to start school before Ben did? It wasn't fair. The delicate melody of "Clair de Lune" floated from the next room where her mother made silver sounds on the golden harp. *Clair de lune* meant *moonlight* in French, and the music sounded like moonlight. Alice should practice, too, right after math homework. Her mother said Alice had perfect harp hands, but Alice's practicing did not sound like moonlight.

The music Alice loved best was Leroy singing with his guitar. Leroy's voice was deep and hungry like wolves calling, and it sent shivers up and down her spine. She wanted to call, too, and run wild. Alice watched wolves running across her mind while the numbers of her math lesson lay flat and dead on the page. Her mother was good at math—classical music and math.

The raccoon waddled through the living room, determined to find the possum and pull its tail for the day's tease. The indoor animals were about ready to go outdoors. In fact, the alligator was leaving the bathtub for a new home in the pond. He was big enough to survive, Alice's mother said, and was not a friendly presence in the house. "One finger too close is one finger gone," warned Alice's father. It would be a relief to have the bathtub back because the shower in the guest bathroom sometimes had visitors arriving through the pipes—centipedes, spiders, or even scorpions that scuttled sideways with raised tails ready to sting. Alice would not get into the shower until her mother checked it for aliens.

She stared out the window and listened to her father snap the pages of his magazine. She heard Ben banging up the back porch. Without pausing, he charged through the kitchen, through the dining room, through the living room door.

"Take off your boots, son."

"There's something wrong with Lucky Jim. You have to come look at him."

"After lunch."

"Right now. His leg's all swollen."

Alice's father pulled on his shoes and rose slowly from his chair beside the radio. Alice abandoned her math lesson and padded after them. The harp music faded away as they left the house.

Lucky Jim's head drooped low. He stood on three legs with his back left hoof barely resting on the ground. Even from the pasture gate, Alice could see how swollen his leg was. Ben began talking to him softly and held out a piece of apple. Lucky Jim nuzzled his hand, but that was all. Alice's father leaned over and looked at the leg. Then he ran a hand up toward the haunch and along Lucky Jim's barrel belly.

"It looks like he's been snakebitten, son, maybe more than once, and the poison's had some time to work. We'll do what we can."

Ben leaned his forehead against Lucky Jim's.

"There must be a nest of copperheads in the pasture

somewhere," said Alice's father, "maybe along this fence. Snakes will look for mice along the old fence holes."

Alice wanted to run away, but she seemed stuck to the ground. She watched her father tend Lucky Jim, then leave for the clinic.

"Can I help, Ben? You want me to bring you anything?" asked Alice.

"Leave me alone," said Ben in a voice so low, she could hardly hear.

Alice retreated to the mimosa tree. From its forked branches, she could just see Ben and Lucky Jim, oddly frozen in the summer air. Late in the afternoon she saw her father stride toward them and bend over Lucky Jim's leg, then shake his head and turn toward the house. Ben did not come in at suppertime or bedtime. Early in the morning, Alice heard her father stirring and followed him outside, down the path to the boy and the horse. Neither seemed to have moved.

"If there's no saving the leg, Ben, there's no saving the horse. You know what I have to do. You might as well bury him right here. Otherwise we'll have to drag his body off with the tractor and dig a hole somewhere else."

As Alice's father set out for the clinic, Ben walked to the toolshed, slumped over like an old man, and brought back a shovel. Then he began digging. Smeared with dirt and sweat, Ben dug hour after hour after hour, until he disappeared into the hole itself.

At lunchtime, Alice's mother ate nothing that she set on the table.

"Why don't you at least let Leroy help him with the digging, Ned. He's just a boy."

"He's got to learn, Lydia. Where there's life, there's

death. The sooner he looks death in the face, the less afraid of it he'll be."

Alice's mother got up and left the table, but her father finished his lunch. Alice went back to her vigil in the mimosa.

Finally, as twilight came on, she saw her father appear with a rifle. Alice slid down the tree trunk, scraping her ankles and legs in her rush to the ground. She fled to her room and buried her head under the pillows and covers. Even so, she could hear the shot. Two shots. And silence.

The Clinic

A week after Ben buried Lucky Jim, school started in town, and Alice hardly saw her brother at all. At meals, he ate silently and then disappeared to do chores or meet his friends. He seemed almost to have left home. Sometimes she went into his room and looked at the photograph of him with Lucky Jim. Ben had moved it from the living room mantel to his dresser, and the picture of him proudly holding the snake around his neck was gone. He had torn it up into little tiny pieces.

Alice did her lessons in the mornings, gathered eggs, and helped her mother with the canning. Bottles of ruby-red tomatoes lined every shelf and table in the kitchen.

"Why do they call it *canning*?" asked Alice. "It should be called *bottling*."

"I suppose because the commercial companies use cans, but that's a good question. Why don't you look up *canning* in the encyclopedia? Speaking of which, we might as well review your spelling while we work. I should give you the placement test tomorrow."

"Okay, ask me some words."

"Encyclopedia."

"That's not on the list!"

"I just thought I'd surprise you. Try it, anyway."

"E-n, en, c-y, cy, c-l-o, clo, p-e, pe, d-i-a, dia."

"Good work! You even divided the syllables right." Alice's mother smiled at her through the steam rising from a huge pot of scalding tomatoes. Her mother's face was often tense with work, but she smiled like sunlight—and she always smiled when Alice did well with her own work.

"I wish I could go to school in town. I read as well as Ben does."

"That's exactly the problem. Ben should be reading much better and much more than he does. The school has no remedial reading program or advanced math, which Ben should be taking, or languages. It didn't even have bathrooms till a few years ago, for goodness' sake! The children had to use an outhouse. The only reason I let him go to school here at all is to make friends."

"I'd like to make some friends."

"I know, Alice. I know how lonely you get sometimes. But Ben's a teenager now, and friends are more important at that age than just about anything else."

"Well, maybe I could go to school during the day and do home-school lessons at night."

"There's not enough time. Something's going to have to change. We can't let you and Ben grow up this way, with a choice between going to school or getting a real education."

Alice retreated from the cloudy kitchen, poking through the house and yard toward the bamboo thicket that her father had planted before she was born. The bamboo spread and curved overhead into a roof of long, delicate leaves that shaded her from sight but let in enough light to read. She settled into the nest she had made and reached into the cast-off bread box that protected her treasures from the rain. Pulling out an old book of fairy tales, Alice curled up to read and spy on people going in and out of the clinic. She could do both at once—she knew most of the stories by heart and hardly had to look at the pages. Probably she was too old for fairy tales, but it didn't matter. Nobody could see her because of the bamboo. Nobody could see that she was the hero, that she feared nothing and journeyed East of the Sun and West of the Moon. Alice opened the book and traveled away with the words.

When she closed her eyes and felt sunlight filter through her eyelashes, she could see the snow-covered mountains East of the Sun and West of the Moon. The girl in the story had been brave to make her way through the world after her father gave her away to a bear. There were no bears in Alabama. No craggy peaks, no prince, no hags, no trolls, but there were talking winds, and someday Alice Ryder would ride them far away. The wind today was soft, rustling the bamboo leaves and moaning through the pines that soared overhead toward pearled clouds and a turquoise sky—south of the sun and moon.

The door of the redbrick clinic opened, and a man limped out on crutches, his wife guiding him toward a battered truck. Together, they managed to get him into the high seat, and his wife drove away. Before they were out of sight, a dusty brown car roared into sight and stopped suddenly. A woman jumped out with a screaming baby and ran through the clinic door, followed by a trail of four other children, each smaller than the last. Her father was going to be busy today.

As the day heated up toward noon, the insects buzzed louder, and Alice heard a hum coming toward her, then the quiet pad of footsteps on pine needles.

"Hey, Leroy."

Leroy whirled around. "What kind of bush is that talking to me?"

"It's me, Leroy."

"Hunh, the Alice Bush, kind of bush that creeps up and scares the life out of somebody passing by minding his own business."

"I didn't scare you, Leroy."

"Look over my head and you'll see the year's growth you just scared me out of."

"You're not growing anymore, Leroy."

"Not for another year, now."

"Where you going?"

"Where does it look like I'm going, carrying this hammer?"

"I don't know, Leroy. We got a lot of buildings nailed together around here."

"Well, Miss Smarty-pants, you're just going to have to guess which one I'm hammering on."

"Can I help you?"

"You got something better to do?"

"Nope."

"Come on, then, if you're not afraid of some hard work. Maybe you can just take over the hammering and I can lie around in the shade all day."

"I don't know which building to pound, remember?"

"You don't know a thing, honey, but that's all right, you'll learn."

Alice put her book in the bread box, crawled out of the

bamboo thicket, and ran to catch up with Leroy.

"Slow down, you're going to bust a gut. Save all that speed for doing my work."

Leroy stopped at the chicken coop and sent Alice to bring a second hammer from the toolshed. Then he boosted her up onto the low roof, scattering the chickens that gathered around his feet looking for grain. Mean Minnie squawked and pecked at him. Leroy handed Alice a pile of shingles, climbed up himself, and began showing her how to pry up the rotten shingles and nail on new ones. They started in the middle and worked away from each other.

"This coop is sure a lot bigger than it looks," shouted Alice.

"Just about every job is," Leroy called back.

After a half hour of hammering, Alice felt like the sun was setting her body on fire. She craved water. When she stopped hammering, Leroy took a long look at her and said, "Go on home, girl, before you pass out. It's a hot day up here on this roof."

Alice nodded her head and climbed down. Then Leroy began his steady pounding again, four beats per nail, bang, bang, bang, bang. Alice could dance to the rhythm of it, but she couldn't keep up with him on a job. Heading toward the house, she stopped beside the spiked fence that guarded the swimming pool and stood staring at the blue-green water. Eerily, she saw the reflection of Ben's face appear beside her in the water.

"Are you home from school already?" asked Alice.

"They let us out early on Fridays."

"Oh, yeah, I forgot today is Friday. It's not fair you get to go to school."

"It's not fair you get to stay home and read fairy tales."

"So what? And how do you know, anyway?"

"You think that hideout is such a big secret."

"Ben, did you spy?"

"I used that hideout before you were even born."

"You were only four years old when I was born."

"I had to hide from you, didn't I?"

"You're just jealous."

"Oh, sure. *I'm* jealous. Of a baby girl."

"I'm not a baby."

"Prove it."

"I don't have to."

"You mean you can't."

"I can do anything you can do."

"Bet you can't cross over that fence."

"You either, Ben."

"I've already done it, Scaredy-cat."

"No, you didn't."

"I did, too, yesterday. Right here where the pipes run from the filter unit."

"Daddy'll kill you."

"He won't ever know. I dare you to climb over the fence!"

The fence rose high over Alice's head. Two pipes, one carrying unfiltered water out and one carrying filtered water back in, stuck through the fence about three feet up. Standing on the pipes, it wouldn't be so far to climb up and over. The thick wire that crisscrossed in a diamond-shaped pattern offered her finger and toeholds. She reached out to test them. Then she pulled herself up onto the pipes and began to climb. When she got to the top, she slung one leg over the long barbs, found a toehold, and slung the other leg over, holding on with both hands while her feet found toeholds down to the pipes. She was almost there. She let go with her left hand as she turned to balance across the last section of pipes to the border of the pool. Suddenly one foot slipped off a pipe and the other after it. For a second she hung by her right hand, then slid downward, but the top spikes caught her hand and raked through it as she fell toward the ditch.

Alice lay there, stunned. She could see her scraped knees clotted with blood and pocked with bits of rock, but it was her hand that hurt. Ben was staring at her hand. Then he was running away and pulling Leroy back toward her, and Leroy was unlocking the gate and half carrying her to the clinic, holding her arm high from the elbow. She was dripping with blood. The bone in her hand looked like a thin white body swimming in a bright red pool.

When they got to the clinic, Leroy rushed Alice past a surprised row of patients in the waiting room and almost ran into Alice's father escorting another patient out of the examining room. He took one look at Alice's hand and turned back into the examining room, steering her inside along with Leroy, who was holding her up, and Ben, who was breathing hard behind them. While Alice collapsed into the big metal examining chair, her father washed his hands and pulled on a pair of thin rubber gloves. Then he sat down beside her with a basin of water and looked carefully at the cut, sponging blood from between the flaps of skin.

"I have to sew up your hand," he said. "Do you want me to put you to sleep, or do you want to watch?" His fierce eyes commanded her to face the pain.

"Watch, I guess," sniffled Alice.

"Good girl."

She did not feel good. Ben and Leroy both disappeared as her father began to move quickly around the room. The examining room also served as his operating room, its walls lined with lighted, glassed-in shelves of medicine and instruments. In the center stood an operating table for surgery, which Alice looked at with dread.

"Stay in the chair, Alice. I'll crank it up a little higher. Miss Taylor is home sick today, but we won't need a nurse. Just hold still." With a pair of gleaming forceps, he took from the sterilizer a needle that looked long enough to spear frogs. Then he fixed it to a syringe, which he filled from a rubber-capped vial, and sat down facing her.

"This will hurt a little till it's anesthetized," he said, and into the gaping pool of flesh he injected the endless needle. Over and over he stuck the needle in. Blood and pain pumped from the wound. Alice scrunched her eyes closed, clenched her teeth, and held her breath against the sobs that were rising from her stomach.

"It won't hurt anymore," he said gently, pressing gauze against the gash. "Just wait a few minutes now while I prepare the sutures." He brought over a curved needle trailing waxed thread.

"Count the stitches," he said. Alice counted fourteen. He was stitching from the inside out as well as bottom to top. His long, tapered fingers in their thin rubber gloves seemed to blend her flesh back together. She watched, almost hypnotized, as he wound a bandage around her hand, washed and salved each knee, and taped gauze over the long scrapes. Just as he finished, Alice's mother rushed into the room.

"Oh, Alice!" she cried. "Look at you!"

"She's all right," said Alice's father. "She was brave, in fact. She watched the whole procedure."

"Ned!"

"Courage takes practice, Lydia."

Alice's parents stared at each other like enemies, gray eyes against blue eyes. Then Alice's mother helped her up, and they started slowly home.

"Give her an aspirin when that anesthetic wears off," called Alice's father.

Alice's mother nodded. "I'm sorry I didn't come right away, Alice," she said. "I was working in the garden, and it took Leroy a while to find me."

Then Alice began to cry. All the tears that had been too surprised to fall at first and too ashamed to fall in front of her father came streaming down like a tropical storm. She walked unsteadily toward the house, leaning into her mother's protective arm. Finally, she could crawl into bed, her face hot and tight from dried tears. Hours later, she awoke to see Ben coming in with a dish of ice cream.

"Fourteen stitches," Alice told him, holding up her hugely bandaged hand. Ben's fine blond hair was damp with sweat, and his blue eyes shifted away from Alice.

"Are they going to punish me for crossing the fence?" she asked him.

"They said you've been punished enough," he said softly. "And so have I."

Then he took his other hand from behind his back, handed her the book of fairy tales, and left the room with his shoulders hunched and both hands in his pockets.

The Pond

"How can I do the workbook if I can't write with my left hand?" complained Alice. "And the essay and the math problems?"

"Did you finish all the reading?"

"I'm way ahead. I've been reading all day—there's nothing else to do."

"All right, Alice, don't complain. You're excused from lessons today. I suppose it won't hurt you to miss a few days of homework, but you'd better start trying to write left-handed. I don't know how long it's going to take that hand to heal. And if you run into Leroy, would you remind him about the alligator? He promised to take it down to the pond a long time ago."

Alice got up, her hand cradled in a cloth sling, and wandered past the morning glories twining around the front porch. Blood-red gladiolas splashed the garden, and verbena in the same color crawled down the low rock wall around it. In the simmering afternoon air, she could hear the distant whine of the sawmill and also something else, a strumming. She followed the sound of the strumming, then humming, and found Leroy sitting on a cane chair in back of the cottage. With one foot hooked on the chair rung, he supported a scratch-scarred guitar on his knee and played, staring out at the trees. His voice did not sound wild today, but far away, like wind hushing through long-needle pines. Deep green, his voice sounded deep green.

"What's that song, Leroy?" asked Alice.

Leroy stopped humming but kept strumming. "I'm talking to myself, is all."

"What are you saying?"

"Just telling myself stories."

"Why are you telling yourself stories?"

"Why are you so nosy?"

"Why don't you tell *me* a story?"

"Honey, most of the stories I got to tell don't belong in your ears."

"Couldn't you make one up?"

"Don't tell me you came traipsing down here to make me make up a story."

"No, my mother wanted to remind you about the alligator. But I do love stories."

"Then why don't you tell me one?"

"I don't know any."

"Well, what is it you read in those books all the time?"

"Oh, fairy tales, but I guess I'm too old for fairy tales."

"Says who?"

"Ben."

"Ben could use a story about now—something to get his mind off missing that horse."

"He wouldn't listen, though."

"Well, I will listen to your story. Just don't make it too long, Miss Princess."

"I'm not a princess, and my favorite story is about a poor girl."

"I bet she turns into a princess in the end."

"Do you want to hear this?"

"Go on, Queen Bee, I'm listening."

"Well, there was this poor girl, and her family didn't have anything to eat. One night they were all shivering by the fire when they heard a knock at the door."

"Watch out, Poor Girl."

"Hush up, Leroy. There's a bear at the door, a white bear."

"Hoo, boy."

"And he says to the father, 'I'll give you anything you want and all the riches in the world if you'll give me your daughter to marry.'"

"Do tell! I hope the father busted him in the chops."

"So the father says, 'Wait a minute, I have to talk it over with her. Come back next week.'"

"Poor Girl's daddy is not right in the head," said Leroy.

"Are you telling this story, or am I?"

"Keep going. I don't like this bear, though."

"The father begs, and the daughter finally agrees even though she's scared to death, and the bear comes back for her, and she packs all her stuff in a handkerchief—"

"Not much stuff."

"And climbs on the bear's back and they travel night and day till they come to a palace—"

"I told you she was going to get royal."

"She's just a lass."

"A what?"

"A *lass*. That's what they called girls then."

"We got better names now, let me tell you."

"Anyway, they live there for a while, but every night a young man comes into the lass's bedroom—"

"Hunh!"

"And she loves him, but she's dying to see what he looks like, especially after her mother tells her on a visit home that she should light a candle and look, which she's not supposed to do."

"Sounds like she's doing a whole lot of stuff she's not supposed to do."

"She sees he's handsome, but the candle spills hot wax on him and breaks the spell that makes him a bear by day and a man by night, so he says he has to leave and she'll never find him till she goes East of the Sun and West of the Moon. But there's no way to get there. Then he disappears."

"Long gone like a turkey through the corn."

"She walks and walks till she meets these three old women. The first one gives her a magic gold ball and and a horse to ride to the second one, who gives her a magic gold comb and a different horse to ride to the third one, who gives her another horse to ride on and a magic gold spinning wheel and some advice."

"Magic gold advice. That's what I need. Three horses wouldn't be too bad, either."

"She has to send the horses back. Anyway, the last old woman sends her to the East Wind to ask him for a ride East of the Sun and West of the Moon. The East Wind carries her on his back to the West Wind, who carries her to the South Wind, who carries her to the North Wind."

"Whoooeee, sounds like a runaround to me."

"The North Wind is so strong, he finally gets her

where she needs to go, East of the Sun and West of the Moon, even though it's so far, it tires him out."

"I'm tired just hearing about it."

"Then the lass finds out her true love is about to marry a long-nosed Troll princess—"

"Ugly!"

"And the lass keeps trying to visit him at night."

"I bet."

"The Troll lets her visit her true love for three nights in exchange for the magic gold stuff, which the Troll wants for herself."

"It's a bribe."

"Right. But every night the Troll puts sleeping pills in his wine . . ."

"This boy is a goner."

"Except the last night, the night before the wedding, he gets suspicious because somebody tells him they heard a woman crying in his room every night."

"Wake up, Buddy."

"This time, he pours the drink out so the Troll can't see it."

"About time."

"The lass gets into the bedroom, and he's awake."

"Mmmhmm."

"The next day he says he won't marry anyone who can't get his shirt clean."

"He's got that right!"

"The Troll wears her fingers out trying to clean up those spots of wax the lass spilled on it—"

"Good luck."

"But the Troll can't do it, and the lass rinses them right out."

"Naturally."

"The Troll gets so mad that she busts open, and the lass and her true love free all the good folk that the Troll locked up—"

"Let my people go."

"And they lived happily ever after."

"Amen."

"Leroy, you are so bad!"

"What did I do?"

"You talked all through the story."

"I talked *to* the story. That shows I was listening."

"Listening means you keep your mouth shut."

"Not to me, girl. Keeping my mouth shut means I've gone to sleep. And I got some thinking to do about this story—now what is it I'm going to need to turn into a prince? Get a girl who loves me and three old women with magic gold presents and three fast horses and four hard winds? Honey, I might as well give up right now. All I got is one old woman who loves me."

"Well, the poor girl didn't have anything to start with, either."

"She was good looking, wasn't she?"

"You're good looking, too, Leroy."

"Do tell! So Mama didn't lie to me about my looks."

"You know she didn't. Anyway, now it's your turn."

"My turn for what?"

"To tell a story."

"All right, all right, we better get on with it. One time, way way back, there was this alligator—"

"Don't tell me how we're going to spend our day and let the alligator go and come back and clean out the tub. That kind of story is for little kids."

"Did you, or did you not, ask me to tell you a story?"

"I did."

"All right, then. Back in those days, Alligator had a white coat he was proud of, mighty proud, downright righteous proud. He was checking himself out in the mirror one day—"

"He had a mirror?"

"If he's got a coat, he's got a mirror. Anyway, he was checking out his reflection in the *swamp water* when he heard a huffing and a puffing and there's Rabbit just about done in.

"'What's wrong with you, Rabbit?' he says. Rabbit says, 'Dog, that's what.' 'Well, that's an old story, Dog chasing Rabbit,' says Alligator. He laughs. 'Not so funny for me,' says Rabbit. He's peeved. 'Tell me something new,' says Alligator. 'How's the rest of the family?' 'Seems like trouble's settled in for a long visit,' says Rabbit. 'Trouble? Who's Trouble?' says Alligator. 'You don't know?' says Rabbit. Alligator thinks for a minute. 'No, I never met Trouble,' says Alligator, 'but I'd like to.' He preens his white coat in the mirror, which is really swamp water but he doesn't know that because some high-hat girl never pointed it out to him. 'I can arrange for you to meet Trouble,' says Rabbit, 'if you come to yonder high-grass field next Sunday, just after sunset but just before moonrise. I'll bring him by.'

"Right on time next Sunday evening, just after sunset but just before moonrise, Alligator grabs his cane and starts prancing out the door when he hears his wife roaring up behind him. 'Where you going, Gator?' roars Mizz Alligator. Alligator roars back, 'Going to meet Rabbit's friend named Trouble.' Mizz Alligator gives him a look.

'Not without me, you're not,' she says, and flicks some cookie crumbs off her own fine white coat."

"Cookie crumbs!" said Alice.

"She just gave the kids a snack," said Leroy. "And here they come. 'Where you going, Daddy? Where you going, Daddy? Where you going, Daddy?' they all screech out. Alligator gives a big sigh. 'Going to meet Rabbit's friend named Trouble,' he says. 'We wanna go, too, Daddy, take us, too!' The little alligators commence to yammering and hollering and jumping up and down, so Alligator caves in and they all file out in their fine white coats and parade over to the high-grass field. And there sits Rabbit on a log right in the middle of the field. No sign of Trouble. 'Where's your friend, Rabbit?' says Alligator, huffing and puffing a little 'cause dry land is not his favorite place. Slows him down considerably. 'He lagged behind a little bit,' says Rabbit. 'You just wait right here and I'll go hurry him up.' Then Rabbit high-tails it over to the edge of the field, stoops behind the bushes, and lights a match to the big old knotty-pine torch he's hidden there."

"A match?" asked Alice.

"Rabbit invented matches and then lost the recipe, so we had to do it all over again," said Leroy. "Anyway, the alligators all line up beside the log and pretty soon they smell smoke. That's not unlikely, 'cause Rabbit's already run in a circle round the whole field lighting up the high grass. Pretty soon, the alligators start feeling kind of warm, warmer than usual on a summer Sunday evening in the swamp, just after sunset but just before moonrise, and they think maybe it's time to go on home and forget about meeting Trouble. They trundle off toward one side of the field, but there's bright red fire licking up the grass that way, so they go to the other side of the field and there's more bright red fire there, and there's bright red fire every which way they turn, north, south, east, and west. The sun slips down and the moon slides up and pretty soon the alligators get so heated up, they just put their heads down and run toward the water, straight south, south of the sun and moon. Of course, to run toward the water, they got to run through the fire, which is also straight south, south of the sun and moon, which is the exact location where they finally meet Trouble and start burning for real. When they hit the water, there's a big huge sizzle. Their white coats crack and turn black and that's the way they still are today. Go look in your bathtub and see."

"Poor Alligator. That's not a very happy ending."

"He got out alive, didn't he?"

"But he got hurt."

"Sometimes it hurts to get out alive. Live and learn."

"Learn what?"

"It depends on the situation. This is a story, not a sermon. If you want to hear a sermon, you better get yourself to church next Sunday."

"And don't go south of the sun and moon—"

"Or if you do, get ready to hightail it out of there. That's it, girl, you've got it. But don't forget what the Good Book says, too, 'The sun shall not smite thee by day, nor the moon by night.'"

"Hey, I know that one—it's from Psalm 121. 'I will lift up my eyes unto the hills, from whence cometh my help.' Then it goes on for a while and then says, 'The sun shall not smite thee by day nor the moon by night.'"

"See how much you learned from your grandmama?

Now we've got to get going if we're going to relocate that alligator."

"Are you going to carry him?"

"How else am I going to get him to the pond? You going to carry him?"

Alice looked down at her hurt hand. She had forgotten all about it. "Won't he bite?"

"Not if I tie up his mouth."

"With what?"

Leroy looked at her white cloth sling.

"Not my sling!"

"That would do just fine."

"It'll get wet."

"It'll dry out."

"It'll get dirty."

"From the bathtub?"

"All right," sighed Alice. "What will I use for my hand?"

"How about your other hand. I'll carry the alligator, you carry your hand."

Leroy laid his guitar on the chair, and they trooped up to the house, past the sunrise-red gladiolas and the sky-blue morning glories, which were starting to close for the afternoon, and into the bathroom. The alligator reared up and hissed as soon as Leroy came near.

"Same to you," said Leroy. "You're going to be sorry you talked to me like that." He unknotted Alice's sling, looped it like a hangman's noose, slipped it around the jagged-toothed jaws, and pulled it tight. The jaws snapped shut. "Watch how you talk, Alice, or you'll be next."

The alligator thrashed its tail and body from side to side. Leroy scooped it onto a big towel and wrapped it up. Then he started quickly out the door.

"That's Daddy's towel."

"Right now I need it a whole lot more than he does." Leroy clamped down on the struggling alligator, which was just about the length of his own arm. Hugging it close to his chest, he walked fast past the garden toward the barn, across three pastures, and all the way to the pond in the woods. Alice trotted along holding her injured hand as still as she could. The alligator seemed to have stopped struggling, but when they got to the muddy bank of the pond and Leroy set it down, the whole towel jumped. Leroy flicked open the thick terry cloth and jerked off the noose. Alice watched the alligator hurtle down the bank into the quiet brown water, like it was looking to cool off from a high-grass fire.

"What if somebody tries to swim in here?"

"Nobody I know is supposed to swim in this pond—what with the tricky drop-off in the middle—and everybody I know knows it." Leroy stared at her hard.

"We don't swim here," said Alice quickly. "Ben fishes in it, and sometimes he wades in the creek up above."

"Mr. Snap-Jaws is more likely to go down the creek if he gets too big for the pond. Anyway, I'll just spread the word there's a wild alligator growing in here. That ought to take care of any visitors for the next hundred years."

"How do you know it's a he?"

"Just guessing from all the hisses I heard."

"Don't females hiss?"

"Naw, females sing and dance the hoola—"

"And hand out cookies to the baby gators, right?"

"Vanilla wafers."

"What if he starves to death?" asked Alice.

"Plenty of little fish in that pond," said Leroy.

"The bathtub must have been pretty awful."

"You just think what it would be like to live in a big white cage all the time, honey. It's a funny thing—he's traveling, now, but he's home free," said Leroy softly, "home free."

The Veranda

Fall cooled off the world a little at a time, week by week, while the bandages on Alice's hand grew smaller each time her father changed them. After he took off the last bandage, a tiny ghost of pain hovered around the wound. The skin had puckered and grown together with a new pink sheen, leaving a white ridge of scar tissue from her wrist to her little finger. Alice was careful with her hand.

"You have to use that right hand, Alice, or it will stiffen up," said her father one morning at breakfast. He was watching her eat left-handed, which she had finally learned to do without dropping half the food in her lap.

Alice wiggled the fingers of her right hand slowly.

"I mean, use it to do things. Don't be afraid if it hurts a little. There's no infection. Here, catch." Her father tossed his car keys across the table. Alice reached out to catch them, but as they fell close, she jerked back and they landed in the scrambled eggs.

"Come on, Alice! You have to try harder than that."

She picked out the keys, wiped them on her napkin, and handed them back to her father.

"Are you going with me on house calls?" he asked.

"No, I'll stay home today."

"Use your hand."

After her father left, Alice stirred the eggs around her plate with her left hand.

"Alice, your daddy's right, you know. Why don't you do some practicing this morning? Just some warm-up scales. That will use your hand without hurting it."

"I don't want to play any scales."

"Well, no need to be grumpy about it. How about an art project? How about starting some Christmas presents? It will be good physical therapy, and we're short on money this year. Besides, homemade gifts are always nicer, anyway."

Alice was silent. She liked store-bought gifts.

"Alice, this has not been a good time for us. Ben's lost a horse he loved and goes to a school he hates. You've been stung and stitched. God forbid that we should have any more disasters. But, meanwhile, we just have to get on with things, and you have to do your part."

Alice got up to clear the table and do the dishes, one-handed, while her mother began making bread. Just the thought of bread cheered Alice up. The dough would rise and rise again and come out of the oven brown and crusty and smelling like Heaven, and they would slice one loaf hot and have it with melted butter and honey.

"I did start making Christmas presents."

"Oh? What are you working on?"

"I can't tell you."

"Well, I guess that's mine. What about Ben and your daddy and grandparents?"

"I don't know about Ben. Boys are hard."

"We're giving him some camping equipment."

"Does he have a canteen?"

"No, he doesn't have anything. All he ever thought about was riding that horse."

"I could find a plastic bottle and attach canvas straps to it."

"That's a good idea, Alice."

"But we'd have to buy the straps."

"We can afford to buy *some* things."

"Good. I was thinking about getting Grandmother an apple peeler."

"An apple peeler! How come?"

Alice shrugged. So, her mother didn't know. Grandmother did not tell on Alice for sinning with the apples. "She needs one, that's all."

"Well, you don't have to make the apple peeler."

"I did have an idea for Daddy, too, and it wouldn't cost much. We've identified all the trees around here, so maybe we should start on wildflowers and order him a paperback guide to take on walks."

"He knows all the wildflowers, too. What about a guide to edible plants? He's keen on survival skills."

"Oh good, I like that."

"You like anything related to food."

"Well, just that, and the apple peeler. And the canteen." And the chocolate almonds. She'd better go gather the eggs if she was going to earn enough to fill the box for her mother. She grabbed the basket.

"What about your grandfather?"

"I don't know. All he ever does is sit there."

"Alice!"

"It's true."

"Why don't you ask your grandmother if she can help you think of something."

Alice charged out the door toward the chicken coop and scared Mean Minnie off the nest, SHOO! The other hens glared at her hand stealing under their soft brown feathers—soft feathers, sharp beaks. Eggs, pennies, chocolate almonds, eggs, pennies, chocolate almonds, eggs, pennies, chocolate almonds.

Alice carried the basket of eggs past the garden, past the bamboo grove, past the pool, and knocked on the screen door of the cottage. A divine aroma sifted through the screen, and flies were fighting to get inside.

"Come on in, Alice, we need those eggs," called Zelda, "but we don't need those flies, SHOO!"

"What are you making, Zelda?"

"Desserts for the clinic trays. Custard and angel food cake. You want some, Angel? All you got to do is wait two hours and they'll be done. I hope."

"Where's Myrtle?"

"Your daddy needed her over at the clinic today. They're real busy."

"What about Leroy?"

"He's out and about somewhere. You could try the barn."

"Naw, I have to go see my grandmother."

"Well, cheer up. That's not the end of the world. I'll tell Leroy you're looking for him."

"That's okay. Just tell him I said hi. And Myrtle, too."

"What about me?"

"Yeah, say hi to yourself, too." Alice piled the eggs into the blue pottery bowl and swung her empty basket out the door, scattering the flies in a buzzing circle. Past the zinnias, withering from lack of rain, past Pixie jumping up and down with every bark like a windup toy terrier. Grandmother appeared at the door as if she had been waiting for Alice.

"Come in, Alice. Come, Pixie!"

"Good morning, Grandmother."

"Your grandfather and I just finished our prayers and Bible reading. He's nicely settled in his chair. Would you like a cup of tea?"

"Yes, Grandmother, thank you."

Pixie stopped barking and trotted around the leopard skin toward the kitchen. She knew the word *tea*. It was the word for doing tricks and getting a cookie.

While the kettle came to a screeching boil, Alice wandered around the house seeking clues for her grandfather's gift. Brass, ebony, ivory, brass, ebony, ivory, brass, ebony, ivory. In his living room chair, with his legs stretched out on a carved footstool in front of him, her grandfather puffed on his cigar and stared at his row of tiny elephants.

"Hello, Grandfather," said Alice politely.

Silence and smoke.

"Alice," called Grandmother. "The tea is ready. Come out to the veranda."

Veranda was another Hindi word. Alice wished her grandmother would just say *porch* like everyone else. She marched out to the screened-in *porch*.

"The veranda's cooler, don't you think?" asked her grandmother.

Alice did not think so, but she sat down politely beside the brass tea tray. From the spout of a teapot that looked like Aladdin's lamp came a stream of amber liquid carefully aimed at each delicate cup. Grandmother had carried her flowered English china all the way to India and then, after thirty years in the mission field, back again to America. Carefully, she poured cream from the little pitcher and offered some to Alice, then dipped a tiny silver spoon into the sugar bowl, one dip for each of them. Alice stirred her tea and took a sip.

"Now what can I do for you today, young lady?" asked her grandmother.

"I'm starting to make some Christmas presents and wondered if you could help me think of something for Grandfather."

"Very thoughtful, Alice, very thoughtful. Giving is the true heart of Christmas. Too many people think only of getting. Now where is my tin of biscuits?"

Carefully she pried open a round tin box of Lorna Doone cookies—the closest she could get to English shortbread—and handed one to Alice, took one for herself, and held one over Pixie's head.

"Sit, Pixie. Now shake hands . . . Now roll over . . . Now dance." Pixie stood on her hind legs and turned around in a circle. "*Shabash!*" said Grandmother. It was her highest word of praise, and she spoke praise only in Hindi.

Pixie sat down and waited with her ears cocked attentively. Slowly Grandmother lowered the cookie onto Pixie's nose. It balanced there for one precarious second. Then Pixie flipped her head, tossed the cookie upward, and caught it in midair like a snapping turtle. The cookie disappeared with a little crunch, and Pixie stood hopefully at attention.

"That's enough, Pixie. Go sit down. Now, Alice, about this pillow."

Pillow, pillow, pillow. Pixie's pillow?

"Well, what do you think?"

"What pillow, Grandmother?"

"Your grandfather needs a pillow to rest his feet on. The footstool is quite hard."

"That's an idea! I could make one for him."

"I thought you could, Alice, and I would be glad to help you buy the cloth and cotton stuffing if you'll do the sewing. Have you finished your tea already?"

Alice was yearning for another cookie, but dared not ask. More than one cookie with tea was a sign of gluttony, and gluttony was a sign of greed, and greed was a sin.

"Yes, thank you."

"Well, you'll be wanting to get along, then. I'll just rob the kitty to sponsor this Christmas present." She pushed herself out of the chair, entered the kitchen through the porch door, and returned with another round tin box just like the one that held the Lorna Doone cookies. From this tin box she pulled out a roll of dollar bills. Alice always wondered how Grandmother knew one tin box from the other. What if she was serving tea to her Missionary Circle and passed around a tin box full of dollar bills? The ladies were so polite, they would probably eat them.

"Here's one dollar, two dollars . . ."—she hesitated—"three dollars! Of course, there might be some change from this, Alice. I'm not sure how much the materials will cost. You may use whatever is left for other presents, if you like. I imagine your egg money doesn't go very far."

"Thank you, Grandmother, that is very generous."

"You're welcome, Alice. Don't wait too long till your next visit."

Suddenly Alice's grandmother leaned over and kissed

the top of Alice's head, a quick peck like a chicken picking up corn. Than she opened the screen door, and Pixie charged ahead like a roaring bull looking for strangers to nip and annoy.

"Come, Pixie," called Grandmother, "come again, Alice."

"I will," shouted Alice. *But not for a while.*

The Store

"I made a list of things I need for the Christmas projects," Alice said to her mother. "Can we go into town today?"

"I suppose so. My sewing needle broke, and I've got to get a new one—there's a huge pile of mending to do. Run over to the clinic and get the car keys from your father. I can't find the extra set. Tell him I'll be back before he has to make house calls."

"We could take the jeep."

"Leave the jeep for the back roads. The Hudson's a lot more comfortable."

Alice tucked the list into her pocket.

"Wait a minute, Alice. Put on some shoes. You can't go barefoot all the time."

"I don't. I wear shoes to church."

"Well, that's a start. Now go do what I asked you to do."

Alice went to her room, buckled on her dusty sandals, gathered her latest egg money, and followed the sidewalk past morning glories, chrysanthemums, and bamboo to the clinic. The air within the thick brick walls always seemed strangely cool. Alice stopped and breathed the smell of rubbing alcohol and cleaning disinfectant that flowed through the door and pooled in the examining room. She liked coming to the clinic when she wasn't coming to get sewed up.

The waiting room was lined with double rows of chairs. Since people without phones couldn't call in, Alice's father did not have an appointment system. The receptionist beside the door seated patients in order of arrival, but the white patients refused to sit with the black patients, and Alice's father refused to have separate waiting rooms. He alternated patients from one side and the other unless there was an emergency. Anybody with bleeding or breathing trouble went straight to the operating room, just in case—as Alice well knew.

Today, both sides of the room were filled. Instead of peacefully pulling and filing charts, Mrs. Daniels at the reception desk was rushing back and forth to answer call bells when the bed patients rang, which meant that Nurse Taylor was busy helping Alice's father in the examining room, which meant that Alice would not be able to see him at all. Several patients looked up and nodded at Alice. They knew her from house calls. Everybody knew the doctor's girl, but they knew her from being sick, not from being friends.

"Hello, Alice, what can we do for you today?" asked Mrs. Daniels. Red-faced and perspiring, she looked ready for bed rest herself.

"Would you mind asking my father for the car keys, Mrs. Daniels? Mother and I are going into town."

"Surely. Wait right here and I'll be back in a flash."

Alice wanted to tell her to slow down, but Mrs. Daniels rolled away like a tractor in high gear and came back jangling the keys ahead of her.

"Thanks, Mrs. Daniels. See you later." Alice ran out the door and all the way home, leaving the patients to be patient.

"I got the keys, Mother."

"I'll be ready in a minute."

"I'll be waiting in the car." Alice ran out to the dark red Hudson, parked so close to the carport pine that she could hardly squeeze through the door. She slipped into the driver's seat and stuck the keys into the ignition, turning the steering wheel back and forth with her good hand till her mother came out.

"Not yet, Alice, move over."

Alice slid across the plush seat as her mother angled in past the pine tree.

"Okay, let's go!" said Alice

"Goodness, Alice, what's your hurry?"

"I haven't been to town for a long time."

"You just want to show off your new scar."

"No, I don't. I just want to do something besides lessons and chores."

"Alice."

"I'm sorry. I didn't mean to complain."

"Then don't."

"Can I get an ice-cream cone?"

"We'll see."

"Look, there's Leroy."

Alice's mother slowed the car. "Do you need anything in town, Leroy?" she asked.

"I want to pick up some things for Mama. Can I get a ride?"

"Surely, pile in."

The heavy car raised trails of red dust on the unpaved road. After a couple of miles, they began to pass houses on the road, and the steeple of the church gleamed ahead. As they whirled past the graveyard, Alice held her breath to keep from inhaling any restless ghosts. The church itself stood small and neat, like the one Alice imagined in "The Little Brown Church in the Wildwood." It was her favorite hymn, and hymns were her favorite part of church, when she could stand up and stretch her legs and sing as loud as possible as long as she stayed on key. "Little Brown Church in the Wildwood" was something she and Grandmother agreed on. They chanted the chorus together like a heartbeat: "Oh *come* come, *come* come, *come* come, *come* come, come to the church in the wildwood . . ."

Past the church came the school. The building was quiet, as if all the children were asleep inside. Alice wondered what Ben did in there all day. It was strange, how he didn't want to go to school. He said his friends stayed out half the time, anyway, to pick cotton.

"Would you rather be picking cotton, Ben?" his father had asked. "I know some families that could use an extra pair of hands."

Ben had turned red and refused to talk about school after that, even if Alice nagged.

The car rolled onto a paved street, past the feed store, past the gas station, past the post office that doubled as a jail, to the hitching post that separated the street from the general store. One single mule waited with a wagon load of hay, switching flies away with its tail and looking lonely behind its blinders. Mules mostly stayed home now. People had cars, or could get rides with a neighbor.

Mr. Henry and Mr. Kyle leaned their chairs against the general store and whittled in the sun. Alice's father called them Salt and Pepper because they spiced up the town gossip before passing it on. Alice jumped out of the car.

"Hey, Mr. Henry, Mr. Kyle."

"Afternoon, Alice, Mrs. Ryder." They said nothing to Leroy, and Leroy said nothing to them.

"Do you want me to check the mail, Mother?"

"Yes, that will save your father from doing it when he goes on house calls. I'll pay for a sack of corn at the feed store, and Leroy can load it for us on the way out of town. We don't want those chickens to go hungry."

"Mean Minnie can go hungry all she wants to," said Alice. She ran into the post office, turned the combination lock on their box, and looked inside. One new package of lessons and three bills. She threw them in the window of the car and watched her mother come back across the street. They reached the general store at the same time. The rusty black screen was decorated with dead flies stuck to a piece of flypaper. Alice pushed it open and pulled out her list.

"Hey, Alice."

"Hey, Mr. Evans."

"What happened to that gigantic bandage you had on your hand a while back?"

"There's nothing but a scar now," she said proudly. "Daddy took out all the stitches. Fourteen. See?"

"Good thing your daddy's a doctor. Think of all the money you saved, at least a dollar a stitch, hunh Mrs. Ryder?"

"Ned charges according to what people can pay, Mr. Evans, you know that," said Alice's mother. "Of course, a good businessman like yourself might have to pay a little more to help support the health of the community . . . but we all know how generous you are."

There was a chuckle from the darkest corner of the store, where Leroy was collecting items for his mother. Mr. Evans stared at him hard. Behind the candy counter Alice smiled, because Leroy called Mr. Evans's place The Stingy Store. Then she stopped smiling, because if Mr. Evans ever found out about it, Leroy would be in trouble.

"Now Alice," said her mother briskly. "Let me see that list. Hmm, we need a length of brown cotton fabric and also black—goodness, Alice, that's a sober color combination—and some cotton stuffing, and by the way, Mr. Evans, I need a packet of sewing needles, medium weight, for a tabletop Singer. And an apple peeler, the best you have. And three feet of canvas strapping, if you carry it. Also, if you have any empty plastic bottles to give away, we'd be grateful."

"I might have some canvas straps at home," said Leroy, walking up to the counter with his hands full, "back from when my daddy was in the army. They're not new, but they're strong."

"Thank you, Leroy. That will do nicely."

Mr. Evans glared at Leroy for cheating him out of a sale. A yard of canvas strapping would have brought half a dollar into the cash register. He pulled down two bolts of cotton, brown and black. The brown looked like chocolate.

"Do you have something lighter, Mr. Evans?" asked Alice. "Kind of a golden brown, like leopard skin?"

"Here's a tan, and here's a yellow, and that's all I've got."

The yellow looked like egg yolk. "I'll take the tan."

"You'll need a yard plus to make a pillow, Alice—I presume that's what the cotton stuffing is for—and what are you going to make with the black fabric?" asked Alice's mother.

"Spots," said Alice.

"I'm beginning to see the plan. Very imaginative. Your grandfather will be delighted." Even being very imaginative, Alice could not imagine her grandfather being delighted.

While Mr. Evans cut the material, Leroy lined up his things on the counter.

"I can pay for my stuff, Mother. Grandmother gave me three dollars, and I have some egg money, too."

"Good for you, Alice, but let Leroy go first. He's been waiting."

"That's all right," said Mr. Evans. "I'll take care of him in a minute."

"I believe that Leroy is first, Mr. Evans. First come, first served."

Several customers browsing among the grocery shelves turned to watch. Mr. Evans's face took on the color of the dark red Hudson. He stuck his hand out for Leroy's money and snapped open a paper bag. Leroy filled the bag, collected his change, and left the store with all eyes on him.

"Now then, Alice, about that ice cream. What flavors do you have, Mr. Evans?"

"Same as always. Chocolate, strawberry, vanilla, and black walnut."

"Black walnut, please," said Alice.

"One scoop," said Alice's mother. "Leroy and I will go pick up the corn, Alice, while you pay for your purchases. Here's some extra money for the needles and the ice cream, and I'll cover the apple peeler, too. Your grandmother shouldn't be paying for her own present."

After her mother left, Alice asked Mr. Evans for twenty more chocolate almonds from one of the glass canisters lined up in a row. Her mother's box was almost full. This batch would finish it off. Mr. Evans wrapped the candy in waxed paper, twisted both ends, and began to add everything up. Just then Alice noticed, at the far end of the counter, a ring of key chains. Almost hidden behind three rabbits' feet was a tiny carved alligator, maybe two or three inches long. The key ring was copper, but the wood was dark brown, with crisscrossed knife marks to show the alligator's cracked-leather back.

"How much are the key chains?" she asked.

"One dollar," said Mr. Evans, "and cheap at the price."

"I don't know. That seems like a lot."

"Take it or leave it."

"I guess I'll have to leave it. I only have ninety cents left . . . unless you can take back some of the chocolates."

Mr. Evans's face tightened up. "Now, Alice, I can't put anything back. That wouldn't be sanitary. You're supposed to know that, being the doctor's daughter and all. I'll tell you what, though. You're a pretty good customer. I'll let you pay me the last dime the next time you come into town. Write me an IOU here, and I'll put it in the cash register."

Mr. Evans handed her the alligator key chain. She wrapped her fingers around it and felt the cool wood, fitted for holding. Then, on a slip of paper, Alice wrote I OWE MR. EVANS TEN CENTS, and signed her name. She burrowed the alligator key chain into the cloth she'd bought, picked up the bulging paper bag in her good hand, and held the ice-cream cone with her bad hand. Mr. Evans turned his attention to the other customers. Nobody watched her go. Outside, Leroy and Alice's mother waited in the car, with the huge sack of corn already loaded in the back end. Alice tucked her paper bag on the floor under her legs where no one could see into it.

"Well, that's that," said her mother.

"I hope so," said Leroy, looking out the window.

"What do you mean?" asked Alice.

"Nothing," said Leroy.

"Let's get on home so your father can have the car and you can start sewing, Alice," said her mother.

"We forgot about the plastic bottle."

"I don't think Mr. Evans has any plastic bottles. I don't think Mr. Evans has *anything* to give away. I'll look around and see what we've got at home."

Alice curled her tongue around the sweet black walnut ice cream that was dripping down the cone toward her scar.

The House

Alice was planning to make the leopard pillow square but after she laid out the fabric, what she saw was a circle, a spot with spots on it. Grandfather probably wouldn't get a sewing joke—or any other kind of joke, either—but at least he could rest his feet on something funny. To heck with his scary old leopard-skin rug. To heck with Grandmother's evil apples. A pillow, a peeler, a pillow, a peeler, a pillow, a peeler. She measured and drew a big circle on the tan fabric, then cut it carefully with sewing shears that left zigzag edges. She sewed the sides together, inside out, on her mother's machine, leaving an open space in the seam to turn it right side out and to put in the cotton stuffing. Then she cut out the black spots. These had to be sewn on by hand, the curving edges of each one tucked under with tiny stitches. It would have been easier if leopards had square spots. Probably no leopard spot was perfectly circular, though, and no two leopard spots quite alike. In the end, the pillow looked more polka-dotted than leopard-spotted, but she had done her best.

The plastic-bottle canteen was easy by comparison.

As Christmas approached, Ben spent less and less time at home, even after school let out. Alice tried to follow him one day, up the rocky road to Leroy's mother's house, but Ben saw her and disappeared into the woods. Alice had to content herself with good company in the kitchen—sugar, shortening, flour, baking powder, salt, eggs, milk, and vanilla. She rolled dough and used cookie cutters to stamp out a parade of animals and birds, each with red or green sprinkles and sometimes both. The oven heated. The green and red animals tanned to a crisp. With cookies cooling on sheets of paper cut from brown shopping bags, the kitchen counters looked like Noah's ark. The house filled with the aroma of cookie.

Ben finally agreed to go with Alice and their parents to find a Christmas tree. He drove the jeep, too, as far as it would go down a backwoods road owned by the lumber company that ran the sawmill. After a long walk and a furious argument, they picked a bright, bushy young cedar, took turns digging it up, and bundled the roots, earth and all, into a burlap sack. Back home, they set it into a tub and decorated the fragrant green branches with gilded walnuts, popcorn, paper chains, and colored lights. They named the tree Emerald. Emerald was going to join the other trees from years past—Olive, Moss, Nile, Fern, Herb, Cone, and company—after the holidays, when they planted it in the cedar grove that Alice's parents had started before she was born.

On Christmas Eve a gray rain spattered against the windows, making their candlelit living room seem like the coziest place on Earth. Emerald sparkled. Alice's mother played Christmas music on the harp. Her father did not even turn on the news, but closed his eyes and listened to the harp. Ben buried his head in old Lone Ranger comic books, but at least he was in the same room. After the last carol, Alice's mother began playing her favorite, "Clair de Lune." With a book propped on the floor, Alice could feel the vibrations of the sounding board. Maybe if God had harps *and* guitars in Heaven, she would go there after all.

The next morning it was still raining. Alice's grandmother and grandfather came in with a big black umbrella, dripping wet, and joined them for tea and oranges and hot buttered biscuits with honey. After that, the family settled themselves near Emerald. Alice's mother and grandparents sat on the sofa, Ben and Alice on the floor. From his armchair by the radio, Alice's father read aloud the name on each gift before passing it along. Ben tore open his presents: a compass, a pocketknife, a mess kit for camping out, a flint-and-steel set to start fires without a match, and the canteen made from a plastic bottle and canvas straps. Alice unwrapped her presents slowly. Two books, *The Wind in the Willows* and *The Hobbit*, which she'd wanted ever since reading selections in her home-school anthology. Two heavy bowls. She looked at her mother quizzically. There were no bowls on her Christmas list. A brush. She did not need a brush. Or a collar. Was it a joke? A leash. And there, wandering toward her from the kitchen doorway, came a fat puppy with huge paws, long ears, and a large red ribbon tied around its neck.

Alice swept up the puppy and rocked it back and forth. Heaven was right here in her lap. A tiny pink tongue licked her cheek and ear. Alice stroked the puppy's head and pulled its ears back from its warm brown eyes.

"That puppy seems to have completely cured your hand," said her father, "a medical miracle."

"Where did you get him? He's beautiful!"

"We called a breeder near Birmingham," said Alice's mother, "and he sent the puppy in a crate with the last truckload of supplies. Ben took care of him at Leroy's cabin so you wouldn't find out."

"That's where Ben's been hiding!" Alice buried her face in the puppy's warm neck.

"He's a cocker spaniel, Alice. They love water. He'll be able to swim with you in the summer," said Alice's mother.

"What are you going to name him?" asked Alice's grandmother.

Alice ran her fingers through the soft curls of fur, bright as polished copper. No, *copper* sounded like *copperhead*. Bright as a golden-red sunrise. "Sunny," she said. "His name is Sunny."

She hardly noticed her mother opening the heart-shaped box that Alice had worked so hard to fill with chocolate almonds, or her father unwrapping the field guide to edible plants, or her grandmother exclaiming over the apple peeler, or her grandfather stroking the soft tan cloth with black spots. They all thanked her and kissed her—except for Grandfather, who seemed quite lost in his pillow—but Alice was busy brushing Sunny and following Sunny toward the kitchen and filling Sunny's dishes with water and food and finding a box for Sunny's bed and lining it with an old blanket. She paid no attention to Christmas dinner, which was her favorite of the year, but excused herself early, leaving Grandmother to help with the dishes and tut-tut about children's manners.

"Oh, let her go," said Alice's mother. "Christmas comes but once a year. And it seems finally to have stopped raining."

With a clear conscience and clearing skies and a dog of her own, Alice ran outdoors. She almost ran into Leroy.

"So, you got a pig for Christmas."

"Oh Leroy, you knew I was going to get a puppy! Isn't he the best one you ever saw?"

"Well, I've seen some good puppies in my time."

"Not like Sunny."

"He's a sweet-looking dog, I have to say that. What do the possum and coon say about it?"

"They're shut up in their cages right now. I guess they'll just have to get acquainted with him. Anyway, they're going back to the woods soon. But Sunny's going to stay forever."

"Old Man Forever can fool you."

"Hey, I got a present for you, Leroy."

"For me?"

"Yeah, I knew you'd come by today." She pulled the tiny package from her pocket. "Here, open it up."

Leroy peeled the tissue paper off and studied the key chain with the tiny carved alligator nestled in his calloused hand. For a long time he didn't say anything. Then he looked up toward the pond. "Home free," he said. "Home free."

"Do you like it?" asked Alice anxiously.

"It's the best gift I got, Alice. But I didn't give you anything."

"You gave me the story. I've still got it."

Leroy looked away again. "And I still got yours, Alice, I still got your magic gold advice—find some poor girl that loves me, three old women, three fast horses, and four hard winds. I'm going to need every single one to get through this world."

"I love you, Leroy. I'd follow you all over the world."

"I wish it was that kind of world, honey." Leroy looked sad as he slipped the alligator into his pocket.

"You going to put some keys on it, Leroy?"

"I got nothing to lock up, just that magic gold advice you gave me."

"Hey, Leroy, we each started out with one story and we each gave one story away, and now we've both got two. It's like a math puzzle."

"You just keep on studying, Miss Brain, and you'll be home free."

Sunny pounced on Leroy's boot laces and started chewing them. Leroy picked up one end of a stick, waving it in front of Sunny's nose. The puppy grabbed the other end and they pulled back and forth, minigrowls leaking out of Sunny's mouth on either side of the stick. When Leroy finally shook it loose and threw it, Sunny ran after the stick as if he'd been fetching all his life.

"Good retriever," said Leroy. "He can bring back all the ducks you shoot in the pond."

"You know I wouldn't shoot anything, Leroy."

"You would if you were hungry enough. Miss Duck makes a fine dinner."

"Sunny can just bring back sticks, that's enough for me."

"Miss stick makes a lean snack."

"Did you eat dinner already, Leroy?"

"Yep, had a fine dinner, but I'm not telling you what it was so you won't cry on my shoulder about what I shot. I came to wish you a Merry Christmas and also ask your daddy to stop up to see my mama again as soon as he's able. She's not doing too well. I hate to bother your daddy on Christmas day, but Mama couldn't even sit up this morning."

Sunny settled down to chew on Leroy's shoelaces again.

"Go ahead in, Leroy. They've finished dinner."

Leroy walked toward the door, shaking Sunny off his foot. Alice scooped up her puppy and headed toward the barn to introduce him to the barn cats, which hissed a hello just like the alligator's. Soon afterward, she heard the jeep start and saw her father roar off into the woods with Leroy hanging on to the roll bar. The jeep was gone all afternoon. When her father came back, he walked slowly toward the house with his brown bag. Alice ran toward him with Sunny tumbling at her heels.

"How's Leroy's mama?" she asked.

"She's holding on, Alice, but it won't be long now till she lets go."

"Leroy will be so sad."

"Leroy will be free when his mother dies, Alice. He can leave here."

"Leroy will leave?"

"He should."

"How come?"

"Because of the prejudice here, that's why. Someday it's going to bring him down."

"But Leroy loves it here. We're not prejudiced."

"We're not the only ones who live here, Alice. Even if it weren't dangerous for a man as proud as Leroy, he'd have a lot more opportunities outside of Shelby County, Alabama."

Alice tried to imagine Shelby County, Alabama, without Leroy.

"Without Leroy maybe you'd even spend a little more time with your grandmother," said Alice's father.

"Maybe." Sunny licked Alice's toes. She reached down to play with his ear.

By the time she looked up, her father was halfway through the back door, and Alice and Sunny were left with the rest of Christmas Day and acres of places to play.

"Come on, Sunny, you haven't met the chickens yet. They won't hiss like the cats, but they'll peck and cluck. You're not allowed to chase them, except maybe Mean Minnie if you don't hurt her. And we'll go see Pixie; he'll jump around and yap. And we'll visit the bamboo nest—you'll just fit in. It might be a little damp, but if it starts raining again, we'll make our own nest in the house, just you and me. We'll make an indoor nest and curl up and read *The Wind in the Willows* all day. You will never be lonely. Or me, either. A house with a dog in it is heavenly."

The Town

The day after New Year's, everybody who had pretended not to be sick over the holidays came into the clinic. The waiting room was packed with a double load of patients, and the sickest ones had to stay overnight so Alice's father could keep an eye on them or treat them or do surgery on them.

"We're running out of everything," said her mother, "and our supplies aren't due from Birmingham for another week. There's not even enough coffee for the lunch trays. Go find Leroy and ask him to take the bicycle into town and pick up a couple of five-pound cans of coffee, Alice. That metal basket on the handlebars will hold them."

"What about Ben? He could drive the jeep. Christmas break's not over till tomorrow, is it?"

"Ben's gone off, goodness knows where, and goodness knows when he'll be back—in time to milk the cows, I hope."

"Ben always milks the cows."

"So far. At least he did the milking before he left this morning."

Alice could tell that the season for peace on Earth was over. Her mother was moving a mile a minute. She braided Alice's hair while she talked, patted her own hair back, and started toward the door. "I'm going over to help your father," she said. "He needs an extra pair of hands today. Mrs. Daniels and Nurse Taylor are frantic. They've got two sterilizers running just to keep up."

Alice closed her math book. "Can I go, too?"

"With me or with Leroy?"

"With Leroy, to town."

"It's all right with me, if you promise to finish your lessons when you get home."

"I will."

"Make sure Sunny's shut up in the kitchen, Alice. He and the raccoon will start playing tag again and tear up the house. Or else they'll give that poor possum a nervous breakdown."

Sunny watched Alice with sad eyes when she closed the swinging door to the kitchen.

"Don't look at me like that. I'll be back soon. Just take a nap."

Sunny lay down with a huff and settled his nose on his wide, furry paws. Alice was almost tempted to stay and play stick with him, but she could play stick anytime. Town was a treat, except for stingy Mr. Evans. Alice took ten cents of egg money to redeem her IOU and then went to look for Leroy. He was fixing a broken fence around the vegetable garden beyond the barn.

"Leroy, Mother says could you go to the store and get a couple of five-pound cans of coffee? And can I go, too?"

"What do you say?"

"Please? Pretty please? Pretty please with cream and sugar on it?"

"Well, all right, since you say it like that. You can go if you sit still on back of the bike and hold on tight. You need a bicycle of your own. You're getting too big to ride behind me."

"I'm getting too big for everything—except the tractor, which I'm not big enough for. I'm too big for the swing! I'm too big for fairy tales! I'm too big for your bicycle! Daddy said I'm too big to be scared of snakes."

Leroy looked down at her for a minute. "Nobody's too big to be scared. You just let your daddy have his snakes and pay him no mind."

"Daddy said Franklin Roosevelt said the only thing we have to fear is fear itself."

"*Who* says *what*?"

"Daddy said . . . that Franklin Roosevelt said . . . that the only thing we have to fear is fear itself."

"Hunh, I can think of a few other things I wouldn't want to meet in the dark." Leroy paused and started to say something else. Then he shut his mouth and marched off to get the bicycle out of the toolshed, with Alice following after him.

The bike raised a cloud of red dust as Leroy peddled toward town, swerving to avoid the squashed frogs and occasional mashed snake that had tried to cross the road in front of a car. Alice tried not to look at them. She closed her eyes and felt the breeze that brushed her face.

"Go faster, Leroy," shouted Alice.

"Hunh! Next time you can peddle and I'll ride in the back."

"I bet I could. I bet I could peddle you home, Leroy."

"How much?"

"How much what?"

"How much you want to bet?"

"I bet you an ice-cream cone."

"Chocolate?"

"Any kind you want."

"How you going to pay for this ice cream if you lose, Miss Moneybags?"

"From my egg money. But remember, I might win. If I peddle you all the way home, you have to treat me next time we go into town."

"And if you get so hot and tired, your tongue starts hanging down to your knees and gets tangled up with the bicycle wheels so you *can't* peddle all the way home, then you treat me next time we go to town, which will be oh so soon. I can taste that chocolate ice cream right now."

"Don't count your chickens before they hatch, Leroy, that's what the story says."

"Honey, don't go mixing up chicken feathers with my chocolate ice cream, that's what I say." Leroy peddled standing up for a while and then coasted. Each curve was a landmark. They passed the graveyard, where Alice held her breath till she got dizzy. They passed the church, where the chorus of "*come* come, *come* come, *come* come, *come* come, come to the church in the wildwood" followed her mind for at least a mile. They passed the school, empty now because of the holidays. They wheeled into town, past the feed store, the gas station, the post office, the hitching post with no mule today, and finally Mr. Henry and Mr. Kyle. Alice got off the bike and stretched while Leroy leaned it against the front of the store.

"I'm just going to see if we have any mail, Leroy. I'll be back in a minute," said Alice.

"I'll just be picking out what size chocolate ice-cream cone I want next time we come into town."

"We'll just see about that."

Alice watched Leroy push against the screen door that led into the store. It wouldn't budge. Leroy pushed harder against the wooden frame. Suddenly the screen door gave way, and Leroy hurtled forward into the dark doorway. Alice heard shouting and ran back to see if Leroy had fallen. He was stooped down, with his arms over his head. Three boys were hitting him with closed fists.

"Stop!" screamed Alice. "Stop it!" She looked around wildly and saw Mr. Evans behind the counter, watching.

"Mr. Evans, make them stop it," cried Alice.

"He started it, Alice, busting in on these boys."

Leroy suddenly pushed one of the boys against another, tore away from the third, and ran out the door. By the time Alice followed him outside, he had disappeared around the corner. Alice's knees were shaking so badly that she could hardly climb on the bike. All the way back, she called and searched for him.

At home, she found him sitting by the kitchen table. Her mother was washing the cuts on his face.

"Leroy, are you hurt bad?" cried Alice. "I tried to catch up with you."

"The road's the slowest way home," said Leroy. His deep voice was hoarse, and he spoke through swollen lips.

"Thank goodness you're back, Alice. Bring me the tube of ointment from the medicine cabinet, and some gauze squares and adhesive tape. Your father's had an emergency call, but he'll be back soon to get his lunch."

By the time Alice gathered the things and returned, her father was walking in the back door.

"What happened?"

"Bunch of kids jumped me down at the store," said Leroy.

"How come?"

"I thought the door was stuck, but they were holding it—and I shoved into them."

"How many were there?"

"Three."

"You know them?"

Alice watched her father check each cut and bruise on Leroy's face.

"They were just kids with nothing else to do, Doc."

"I asked you, Leroy, do you know them?"

"Sure, I know them, but I'm not looking for any more trouble."

"You've already got it whether you want it or not."

"Look, Doc, I could have taken down all three of those little"—Leroy stopped and looked up at Alice's mother—"Well, I won't say what they are. But if I'd done it, I wouldn't stay alive long to tell about it."

"No, you did the right thing, coming back here. But if we let them get away with this, it'll be just the start. First you won't be able to go into town, then you won't be able to go home at night."

Leroy winced as Alice's father smoothed adhesive tape over a cut across his cheekbone.

"What did they use on you? These are not just fist marks."

"Doc—"

"Let's go, Leroy. I want you to come back into town

with me and identify them for the sheriff. Do you think your mother will be safe by herself in the woods if we don't settle this?"

Slowly, like an old man—like Alice's grandfather, or Ben digging Lucky Jim's grave—Leroy dragged himself out of the chair. Alice's father unlocked a wooden cabinet in the kitchen, pulled out his pistol, and dropped it into his pocket.

"We'll be back, Lydia."

"Ned, if you're going, I'm going."

"Don't be foolish."

Alice's mother took off her apron. "I'm not the one being foolish. There's less likely to be a confrontation if your family's there. I'm coming, and Alice is coming, too. If you put that gun away, we can settle this peacefully."

"Speak softly and carry a big stick."

"Nonsense! You're not Theodore Roosevelt. We're dealing with a small town and people we know."

"We may not know them as well as you think."

"We've lived here for years!"

"Lydia, you're still a Yankee, and I was born farther away than anyone in this town has ever been. We'll always be outsiders."

Alice's parents climbed into the front seat of the Hudson, Leroy and Alice into the back. The car seemed to eat up the road that earlier had stretched out so slowly under the bicycle wheels. When they got to town, the first thing they saw was a knot of men buzzing around the general store like wasps. Alice's father unfolded his long legs from the car and nodded to the sheriff, who drifted down the board sidewalk toward him with a half wave, half salute. Alice's father went to meet him. Alice's mother, her lips tightened in a hard line, opened the door on the passenger's side to get out, too. Alice and Leroy sat still. The air seemed to crackle like the eerie green electric sky right before a tornado.

"Now, Doc," said the sheriff. "There's no call for you to get mixed up in this."

"Three boys attacked my employee, Tom."

"That's not the way they tell it. They say he pushed into them and hit out. We don't hold with that kind of thing. Leroy Jackson is too big for his britches. He's been needing a reminder of that for a long time."

"If anybody touches him, Tom, it will be over my dead body."

Mr. Kyle and Mr. Henry looked down at their whittling knives. One of the farmers who lived off the highway past town reached into his open truck and pulled out a tire iron. He stepped up behind Alice's father.

"Ned!" cried Alice's mother. Alice watched frozen from the backseat of the car. Then a little movement rippled through the group as a tall man in a brown uniform slammed out of the store and another man in uniform followed him.

Alice's mother climbed back into the car. "Thank God! Somebody called the state police," she whispered. Leroy said nothing, but Alice saw his hands clench and unclench, clench and unclench.

The tall man shouldered his way toward Alice's father and led him aside. "I'm taking your boy with me. He'll be safer that way. There's going be a lynching if we don't get him out of here."

"You're putting *him* in jail? What about the boys who beat him up?" demanded Alice's father. "Leroy Jackson has been my employee for years. I swear he has better sense than to start anything like this."

The patrol officer opened the car door and snapped handcuffs around both Leroy's wrists. "Look, I'll guarantee full protection to Birmingham. When we get there, I'll even put him on a bus anywhere he wants to go. But if we don't make it look like an arrest, I can't guarantee anything."

Leroy looked at Alice's father. "Take care of Mama," he said. Then he turned and got into the police car. Alice, her mother and father, and the group of people around the store all watched them drive away. The silence was thick as red dust on an August road. Alice's mother stared ahead as if she saw nothing. Alice's father looked carefully at each person standing beside the store. He had delivered their babies and set their broken bones and taken their blood pressure and listened to their hearts. No one looked back at him. Finally, he started the car and set off for home.

The Journey

It took Alice's parents seven months to sell their land. January, February, March, April, May, June, July passed, and in all that time, Alice could count the changes on the fingers of one hand.

Leroy's mother died, with Alice's father by her side.

Alice's parents took trips looking for a new place to live.

The raccoon and possum returned to the woods.

The broken-winged owl healed and flew away.

Sunny grew.

Everything else stayed the same. Then, in August, everything changed. Alice's mother sold Brownie, Patch, and all the chickens. After that, she packed up the house. Alice felt like an empty eggshell.

"What will Grandmother and Grandfather do?"

"They'll be all right, Alice. This is their mission field now. It would hurt them more to move than to stay. Change gets harder when you're old."

"Won't they miss us?"

"Of course, but we'll visit and write and telephone."

"I don't want to move."

"It's too late for that, Alice. The time has come to put one foot in front of the other. Besides, it will be exciting once we get there." Alice's mother wrapped the last of the china in torn pieces of newspaper. Her face, smudged with black, was damp from the noon heat.

"Wait till you see our new house on the mountain, and the lights of the city spread out over the valley, and your school, and the stores downtown."

Alice thought about Mr. Evans's store. She had not been in it for seven months. She would never, ever pay him back the last ten cents for Leroy's present.

"They even have snow sometimes in east Tennessee," said her mother, "and bears in the Smoky Mountains."

But not white bears, thought Alice. I'll still be south of the sun and moon.

"And you'll have friends."

Friends.

"Did Daddy hear anything about Leroy?"

"No word since the one postcard you saw. I'm not sure he stayed at that address. We should have heard back from the letter we sent about his mother. Maybe he's just too heartsick to write."

"He must know his mama died, or he would have come back."

"Sometimes I think she died so he wouldn't have to come back."

"But Daddy said she had cancer."

"That's true, Alice. She died because she had cancer . . . but a broken heart never helps."

"How will he know where to find us?"

"I don't know that he will, Alice. Some stories are just about too sad to bear."

"Poor Alligator. That's not a very happy ending."

"He got out alive, didn't he?"

"But he got hurt."

"Sometimes it hurts to get out alive. Live and learn."

"Learn what?"

"It depends on the situation. This is a story, not a sermon. If you want to hear a sermon, you better get yourself to church next Sunday."

"And don't go south of the sun and moon—"

"Or if you do, get ready to hightail it out of there. That's it, girl, you've got it. . . ."

"The moving van is coming at seven in the morning, Alice. Have you checked your closet to make sure you got everything?"

"I did." Her bamboo hideout was empty, too, the fairy tales nestled in her overnight bag.

Alice walked from the house to the barn, with Sunny running ahead of her. The copperhead was a long, bony skeleton now. Sunny gave it a sniff and ran on. Alice walked to the barn, climbed into the loft—holding her dog cradled in one arm—and looked out past the pasture where Lucky Jim was buried and past the pond where the alligator lay in the mud, to the clinic and beyond, to her grandparents' house where the wasps nested. She looked away from the cottage where Myrtle and Zelda had teased her since she was born, away from the hole in her heart where Leroy lived. Such a heavy sadness settled on her shoulders that she could hardly straighten them up. She dropped her eyes and watched dust motes turn the slanting sunlight into a ghost slide.

The only sound was Sunny's rush around the loft to smell each spot where some mouse or rat or bird or bat had been. Alice finally gathered him up in her arms, a bundle of curly fur, and settled him beside her.

"You're going with us, Sunny, don't worry. You'll be with us all the way."

Sunny struggled to run off and investigate one more mouse hole. Alice, with tears slipping down her face, fell asleep in the loft for the last time.

Part II

TENNESSEE, 1955-56

The Yard

Unpacked boxes piled high around them like pyramids of cardboard. Alice helped excavate their bed sheets, pajamas, and toothbrushes, then sat down on one of the boxes to eat cheese sandwiches. Sunny wandered from one pair of feet to the next, snuffling up fallen crumbs. When he had vacuumed the whole floor, he begged silently, resting his chin on Alice's knee and gazing at her. Through his soulful brown eyes shone a clear message: Alice, I am deeply hungry. She took the hint and found his bowls, filling one with dry dog food and the other with water. He sniffed them and looked at her reproachfully. Neither bowl contained cheese.

"Tomorrow and Sunday, we'll unpack," said Alice's mother, "and on Monday we'll enroll you both in school."

The bite of apple Alice had just swallowed turned a somersault in her stomach. School was one of the reasons they had come here. School was what she'd always wanted. Now she had no choice. Monday was laid out like a map with four roads. Her mother would go to symphony rehearsal, her father would walk down the mountain to his new clinic, Ben would walk over the mountain to his military academy, and Alice would walk along the top of the mountain to a public school. That was her road. Even Sunny was going to follow trails of his own through a dog door engineered by the previous owners. He'd already tried it out several times. Alice knew that the family had always gone their separate ways, but these new ways were unknown. And this new kingdom was larger than her old one, much too big to view from a barn. She did, though, have a safe perch, a tiny sunporch she had claimed for her bedroom on the top floor of their odd-shaped, four-story house. The old wooden house climbed up a mountain so steep that the yard was terraced like a staircase. Everything in the mountains and in their house went up and down.

"You'd better get your bed made up, Alice," said her mother. "It's been a long day."

Alice gathered her things together and called Sunny away from the tantalizing whiffs of cheese that still wafted around the packing boxes. He trailed her like a short, fat shadow up the steps to her room, which already seemed familiar. With nearly floor-length windows on three sides and bookcases on the fourth wall, there was just space for a bed, a small dresser, and a round rug on the wooden floor. It was cozy as a bird's nest lined with down feathers, and from it she could look out through the treetops. Her new nest was just an arm's length from the squirrels that leaped along the branches right outside her windows. Sunny was keenly interested in these squirrels and claimed the bed as the best observation post. Alice could not get the sheets on properly with a lump of dog in the middle. Finally it was done and they settled down to squirrel-watch till nighttime. Personally, Alice found the blue jays, doves, and cardinals more interesting—there was even a woodpecker pounding on a tree trunk—but dogs deserved their own hobbies. Lying in bed as the sky darkened, with Sunny curled up beside her, she could see lights coming on in the valley far below and felt a world of possibilities stretching before her.

On Saturday morning, the rising red sun woke her. Quietly, she tiptoed down the stairs and outside to explore, before her mother could call her back to spend the day unpacking. Sunny padded after her on his quiet paws, furry as a hobbit's. Occasionally he raised a back leg to pee where he sniffed interesting places. On either side of the steep yard stretched a small patch of woods, with oak trees sturdier than the tall, slender pines Alice had left behind. Instead of a soft bed of pine needles, acorns cracked underfoot. And instead of dusty kudzu vines, the terraces were covered with ivy and wild rosebushes. Maple leaves and mountain ash whirled in a carnival of early fall colors. Sunny dashed back and forth with a stick, then sat down to chew on it.

Suddenly, Alice stopped. Ahead of her, on the edge of the highest terrace, dangled a long brown rope that for a minute looked like a snake hanging from the thick branch overhead. The rope was knotted at shoulder level and again at ankle level. Alice pulled on the rope, then hung on it with her whole body. The branch was so strong that it hardly dipped. Alice backed up, wrapped her hands around the upper knot, ran forward as fast as she could, and swung out over the incline below. The bottom knot made a footrest as she soared out and back, out and back in the leaf-filtered light. Her flight through the air created a little whoosh of wind. All she had to do, to travel the unknown land, was hold on with all her might.

The School

On Monday morning, Alice's father walked her to school. The road, once a streetcar track winding along the ridge and down the mountainside into the city below, was tarred and graveled now, but still narrow. Not many cars passed by. The houses and yards were large, and the roadside was heavily wooded. Sunny's ears were already matted with burs from the bushes where he ran off to chase rabbits and chipmunks.

"What's that tree, Alice?" asked her father.

"Maple?"

"Sycamore. Look at the leaf again, and the white bark. You've got a whole new world to get acquainted with up here."

Alice dropped her head back to look at the top branches of the sycamore tree. Was *up here* two states north of Alabama, or the top of the mountain? The same sky covered everything, but the air was different here. The air was cooler.

As they approached the school, they passed children first in ones and twos, then in groups that buzzed and swarmed. Some ignored her and some stared. For the first time, Alice, who had been trying to catch up with Ben all of her life, felt too tall. She bent over like a lone pine leaning in a hard wind.

"Stand up straight, Alice," said her father.

Alice pushed her shoulders back and leashed Sunny to a tree, where he flopped down panting. The noise swelled on the steps into the school, and two huge doors swallowed them into a hive of strangers. Alice's father found the principal's office, spoke with the assistant, and signed some papers. Then he squeezed Alice's shoulder good-bye and left to walk Sunny home again.

"Follow me, dear," said the assistant.

They dove into a current of students streaming down the hallway to a room that said MISS SIMPSON, FOURTH GRADE.

"Here we are," said the assistant.

"But I've finished all the fourth-grade work, and most of the fifth grade, too. I'm in eighth-grade reading."

"What school did you say you went to before?"

"My mother taught me at home."

"Oh, you're the home-schooled girl. Well, those records were very confusing. We'll just try you out here and see how you do."

The students who had already settled into their seats all turned to peer at Alice, and Miss Simpson rushed over to show her an empty desk. As Alice squeezed into it, a girl across the aisle said in a chicken-squawk voice, "You're too big to be here."

Silence dropped on the room like a bomb. Alice tried to blend her body into the chair, but there was no hiding from a whole classroom full of eyes. Miss Simpson called the class to order and handed out math sheets. The problems were easy. Alice settled down to work. Twenty minutes later, the principal's assistant returned to the doorway and beckoned Alice back into the hall.

"You're supposed to be in fifth grade," she said sternly, and led Alice to another classroom, this time through hallways echoing with emptiness. Everyone else was where they belonged.

The fifth-grade teacher who came to the door was tiny, lean, and leathery looking. Her eyes fixed on Alice like magnets to metal.

"This is Alice," said the principal's assistant. "We had a little mix-up this morning as to which class she should be in."

"Well, Alice, I'm glad you've finally arrived at the right place. My name is Mrs. Hopkins. Please take the empty seat by the fish tank. I trust you like guppies. We'll make you a name tag later, but everyone can remember Alice, of course, from *Alice in Wonderland*. As a matter of fact, we're just starting the new year with some writing."

Two boys in the back row snickered. Alice felt as if she had suddenly grown ten feet from eating a Wonderland mushroom. She walked the new gauntlet of eyes and sat down. The desk was just barely big enough.

"Now!" said Mrs. Hopkins, gazing out the window. She seemed to have eyes in her ears and did not have to face anyone to command attention. "I want you all to look at the picture above my desk."

Fifty eyes pivotted to the picture above Mrs. Hopkins's desk.

"Imagine," she said, "that the scene there has come to life and is part of a story unfolding. I want you to write that story."

Alice stared at the teacher, standing dwarfed under the painting of a shadowy figure who paddled a canoe through dappled shade. What story was Mrs. Hopkins talking about? Alice could hardly even see the shadowy person, or tell whether it was a man, woman, boy, or girl. Was he—or she—hiding, or slipping along the shore to spy on someone? Was it morning or afternoon? Alice looked out the window while everyone around her started chewing pencils and bowing over rectangular sheets of paper. Finally, she made her way up to Mrs. Hopkins. Alice was tall enough to whisper into her all-seeing ear.

"I don't understand what you want us to write."

Mrs. Hopkins's eyes were dark, dark brown. "Anything you want."

"Anything?"

"Anything."

"About the picture?"

"About the picture."

Alice walked back to her place beside a boy whose name tag said, JIMMY BRECKINRIDGE. Jimmy Breckinridge seemed unable to sit still for more than two minutes at a time. Already he was squirming forward to drop an eraser down the gap formed by the winged shoulder blades of a girl whose name tag said MARY JANE McCALL. Without a pause in her writing, Mary Jane McCall crooked a thin arm down her back, retrieved the eraser, and dropped it on the floor. It bounced with two tiny sounds, thud-thud.

"Jimmy." Mrs. Hopkins did not even look at him, but his name rang out like cracking timber. Jimmy picked up his eraser and applied it so vigorously that his paper tore.

Alice drifted back to the picture. Ideas began to float her down the stream with the canoe. The shadowy figure was a girl. She had a mother, a whole family, but she was separated from them. She was alone and afraid. Her only hope was to be quiet and skillful with the paddle. It was twilight, the air as blue as the water. Alice was rippling along when Mrs. Hopkins called a halt to their work. It was time for recess. Alice had not written one word and had nothing for Mrs. Hopkins to check, but she had started traveling and knew she would go again. She was sure to meet that girl in the picture and find out what happened to her. Maybe tonight.

Alice followed the others out to the playground for recess. They peeled off into groups—ballplayers, marble shooters, rope jumpers, swingers, sliders, jungle-gym climbers, show-offs, gossipers, and loners. It was like a county fair with contests, and Alice could tell that each person was judging or getting judged. A blue ribbon here, a red ribbon there, a yellow ribbon, a white ribbon, no ribbon. Everybody wanted to play with the winners, which meant that nobody wanted to play with the losers. There was no bamboo hideout from which she could spy and stay unseen and imagine her brave journey through the world.

Alice felt too tall again, the lone-pine-leaning-in-the-hard-wind feeling. No, it was worse this time, a-lone-pine-leaning-in-the-hard-wind-and-about-to-be-struck-by-lightning. She could feel a storm brewing. Nobody came near her. She watched Jimmy Breckinridge watching her and then she watched him whisper into another boy's ear. What was the other boy's name? Dick Burkhart, D. B., Dumb and Big. Alice moved closer to the playground monitors—two volunteer mothers who wore white canvas chest straps—and stared at her own feet so she wouldn't have to look at anyone else. The heavy brown oxfords that her parents had bought her for the new school year looked like tree roots.

Alice raised her eyes and saw the feet around her, penny loafers on the girls and sneakers on the boys. She could stay on this playground a thousand years and still look strange. The mothers on this playground did not buy heavy brown oxfords. They bought penny loafers for the girls and sneakers for the boys, and it looked like they all bought them at the same store. The mothers on this playground probably all had their babies at the same hospital, where the mothers made friends with each other and the babies made friends with each other. That was the secret of winning a blue ribbon. Getting picked for teams started at birth and ended at the shoe store.

The bell rang while Alice was still staring at shoes. She did not see Jimmy and Dick crowd behind her until too late, when she was being squeezed like an orange. Alice jabbed each one with an elbow. The boys reeled away.

"Peeyew, she stinks," shouted Dick.

"You're gonna die, Dick," said Jimmy.

"You, too, Jimmy, you're gonna catch it, too. She's spreading her smelly germs all over!"

Ducking away from Alice's smelly germs, the boys blended into a raggedy line that was forming to enter the schoolhouse. When Alice moved to change places, a blond girl pushed her back and said, "Hey, no budging." Trying hard not to cry, Alice dropped to the end of the line and waited to go in. The problem was much bigger than shoes and mothers and strangeness and tallness. There was something else about her, something different right through to the heart. The other kids knew it right away. They knew it, and she knew it.

✣ ✣ ✣

"They're just bullies," said her mother. "Don't pay any attention to them and pretty soon they'll get bored and leave you alone."

"You have to fight back," said her father. "If you don't, they'll hound you forever."

"Just show me who they are," said Ben grimly. "I'll take care of it."

None of these things would work. How could somebody not pay attention when somebody else was chanting *nyanh-nyanh-nyanh-nyanh-nyanh*, or pointing a finger that slipped into jabbing somebody's back, which Jimmy and Dick did to her the whole week? And how could she fight them? Ben couldn't be her bodyguard. If only she had a friend for protection. But she didn't, and torment was contagious, *nyanh-nyanh-nyanh-nyanh-nyanh*. Nobody else wanted to catch it, *nyanh-nyanh-nyanh-nyanh-nyanh*. Nobody wanted to risk being friends with an enemy of Jimmy and Dick, *nyanh-nyanh-nyanh-nyanh-nyanh*. Alice was quarantined to keep from spreading *nyanh-nyanh-nyanh-nyanh-nyanh*. Still, at the end of the fifth long day at school, she went home to find an invitation to Mary Jane McCall's birthday party. Everyone in the class was invited. Alice knew because Mary Jane had said so to everybody who'd begged to come. Miss Princess.

On a crisp Saturday morning seven days after she got the invitation, Alice laid out her silky green Sunday school dress and white socks. She cleaned up her summer sandals with messy white shoe polish that dripped down her fingers. She longed for a pair of black patent leather shoes with pointed toes. People's toes were not pointed, her father said, until they forced them into pointed shoes and got foot trouble. She washed the shoe polish off her hands and wrapped up the book she had picked out for Mary Jane's present, *The Wind in the Willows.*

Alice's mother drove her to the McCalls's house at exactly 1:30 P.M., when the party was supposed to start. Swarms of dressed-up classmates, looking nothing like their everyday selves, clutched fancy packages as they climbed out of their parents' cars.

"I'll pick you up right here at four o'clock. Don't be nervous, dear. You know all these children from school. You'll be fine," she said. "Just be yourself." Alice looked out the window. Being herself was a disaster. If only she could be somebody else. She got out and faced the long sidewalk into Mary Jane McCall's house. Through the door spilled the sound of a musical-chairs game already in full swing. Aside from a little pushing and shoving, Alice survived this with surprising ease. Mrs. McCall was class mother, and she organized the group like an army officer marshaling troops from one action to the next. The pink-and-white sandwiches, the pink-and-white cake, the pink-and-white ice cream, and the pink-and-white fizzy punch presented no problems. There was some tittering when Mary Jane unwrapped *The Wind in the Willows* and Jimmy whispered "baby book," but Alice slipped into the bathroom and by the time she came back, the last present was drawing oohs and aahs. The clock said 3:00. Mrs. McCall was picking up sticky pink-and-white plates and beginning to look tired.

"Why don't you take them outdoors, darling," she said to Mary Jane. "You can all play outside together till the parents come. Maybe you can even take turns on the pony."

Everyone dashed for the back door in playground formation while Alice trailed behind, just as she did at recess. They swarmed around the shaggy, snow-white pony and patted it and begged for rides. The pony was round and gentle. He carried each rider who clambered on his back for a circle around the yard—like the white bear in "East of the Sun and West of the Moon," thought Alice. She stood at the end of the line. It was hard to wait. Finally her turn came and she stepped up to the pony.

"Wait," said Mary Jane, "you can't ride him, Alice. You're too big."

"I'm not," said Alice. "I'll sit very still."

"My father said not to let anybody too big get on my pony. It will hurt his back."

"She's taller than the pony. She'll squash him like a bug," shouted Jimmy, circling back for a second turn.

Alice turned away. She would not cry here, she would not. But tears were already clogging her eyes, and there was no shelter in sight—only smooth lawn, white fence, and trim house. *"Don't go south of the sun and moon. . . . Or if you do, get ready to hightail it out of there. That's it, girl, you've got it."* Beyond the valley rose the mountain where she lived. Alice slipped out the back gate and ran toward it. After a while, she slowed down and stopped crying, but her head ached with every step. The valley was wider than it looked and crisscrossed with roads that turned into streets as she passed through a new housing development edging the city. Uncertain which way to go, she walked for hours with the white sandals rubbing her feet. Shadows darkened as she trudged uphill. Finally, she rounded a curve and recognized familiar landmarks—the sycamore trees that lined the road between school and home.

It was eight o'clock when she walked in. Sunny wagged his tail violently. The rest of the family sat at the kitchen table, with dinner cold on their plates. "Where have you been?" exploded Alice's father, pushing his chair back. "We've got the police scouring the whole countryside for you." Ben sidled away through the door, leaving her with nowhere to look except the linoleum floor.

"I got lost."

"Why did you leave the party?" asked her mother. "I told you I'd pick you up."

"They wouldn't let me ride their pony." Even to Alice, this sounded so lame that she could hardly tell them what happened. It came out in bits and pieces after she retreated to her room in shame, undressed, and got ready for bed.

"I'm sorry, Mother. I didn't mean to cause so much trouble." By now, even Sunny could tell something was wrong. He watched her dolefully from the floor, with his head between his paws.

"Well," said Alice's mother, "I can see why you were hurt, but don't ever run away again. You gave us a real scare."

"Did Daddy really call the police?"

"He did, and I'm calling that girl's mother right now."

"Don't call," begged Alice.

"I have to. They need to know you're safe. I think the girl's parents should know why you left, too."

"No, please. It will make everything worse. Just tell them I'm home."

Alice's mother shook her head, turned out the light, and left the room. That was the signal for Sunny to jump up on the bed. She threw her arm around him. "You should have been there, Sunny. You should have seen the white pony." Tears began to leak through her eyelashes again, and Sunny promptly licked them off. But Sunny couldn't go to parties and playgrounds.

Maybe, thought Alice, the only friend she'd ever have would be the dark girl in the picture over Mrs. Hopkins's desk. The headache that had stayed with her all the way home from the party now thumped against the pillow. If she lay very still, she could keep the pain in one place. Alice lay very still.

The Road

Every morning Alice's father walked her to school with Sunny, and every afternoon she walked home alone. Unlike Alabama, mornings were cool, but afternoons were still hot. She was not sure when Jimmy Breckinridge and Dick Burkhart had started following her after school, but the rock throwing began with a little piece of gravel from the road. It hit her right in the middle of the back, a light tap. She looked around and saw nothing. An acorn? Sometimes acorns fell. She shifted her schoolbooks from one arm to the other and kept going. The next time, a fistful of gravel sprayed across her back. Alice began to run, books and braids swinging, pebbles pinging behind, September sweat beading her red face. Her breath came in spurts, and she could hear laughter behind her. The math book slanted sideways and fell, then the geography book. Her library book and notebook began to slip from under her arm and dropped. Finally she could go no further. She stopped, turned, and faced her tormenters.

Pelting along full tilt, Jimmy almost ran into her. Alice

pushed him away. Jimmy shoved her back. Dick danced around them. "'Fraidy cat . . . She's afraid to fight. . . . Fight her, Jimmy, she's as big as you are." Jimmy took a tentative swing, and Alice flailed back. His fist bounced off her eye. Her first punch went wild, the second landed somewhere on his shoulder. Both of them punched the air near each other, backed off in a heavy-breathing halt, and stared. Dick jumped around slower and slower, like a windup toy with no one turning the key. He was already getting bored.

"Come on, Jimmy, let's go. She's just a dumb girl." Jimmy allowed himself to be herded back the way he had come, throwing rocks at the sycamore trees and throwing shadow punches at Dick.

Alice finally picked up her books, hands shaking, and trudged toward home. By the time she got there, her eye had swelled and was turning a strange color. Worse than that was a headache starting up again. She could hear her mother practicing intently when she came in. Suddenly, in the middle of an arpeggio, the music stopped.

"What happened to your face?" cried her mother as Sunny circled and wagged around Alice's feet.

"I had a fight."

"Oh, Alice!"

"With those boys."

Her mother got up and held her close, then stepped back and looked at her. "What are their names?"

"Don't call them. Don't call anybody."

"We'll see. Let me get you a cold washcloth. You're going to have a black eye—this is terrible. We came here so you could go to a good school."

"It is a good school. Mrs. Hopkins is wonderful."

"But the children are cruel to you, Alice. It's so unfair."

"They don't like me."

"They don't even know you."

Alice shrugged. "It's the same thing."

"You need to lie down. You're pale as a ghost."

Alice looked through the window at the thick oak trees. "I'm going out to swing on the rope."

"Oh, Alice, not now."

"Please."

"Don't you want to clean up and rest first?"

"No, I just want to swing."

"All right, then, but be careful."

"The rope is safe," said Alice. "Daddy said so." As she walked out the door with Sunny racing ahead, she heard her mother pick up the interrupted passage of music on her harp. Her mother never gave up on the hard parts.

The wind from swinging felt wonderful on her face. With each lift off the ground, her headache lifted, too. Back and forth, back and forth, she hurled herself out into space over the terraced yard while Sunny barked at the bushes lining the empty lot beside the house. Those bushes looked like they might make a hiding place—not as good as bamboo, but the branches curved over to make a leafy cave. Alice dropped off the rope swing, wandered over, and stuck her head through an opening in the thicket. A green shirt flashed in front of her.

"Hey!" called Alice.

The shirt stopped, but did not turn around. Sunny bounded forward.

"I surrender," said the shirt with arms held high in the air.

"What?"

"I surrender."

"Why do you surrender?"

"Because I'm a spy for General MacArthur, stupid."

"Come on, who are you really?"

"I don't have to tell you anything except my rank and serial number."

"Well, okay, tell me your rank and serial number."

"Do you want to play General MacArthur?" The green jacket turned around. Above it was a face with hazel eyes and a camouflage hat. The camouflage hat was stuffed with long red hair that escaped in straggly curls.

"How do you play?"

"Well, see, General MacArthur is the hero. My father says General MacArthur was the real hero of the Korean War. My father says he should have been president of the United States."

"But how do you play General MacArthur?"

"See that great big drainpipe that runs under the road? We crawl through that and evade the enemy."

"Who is the enemy?"

"That depends. Sometimes it's soldiers and sometimes it's cattle rustlers and sometimes it's the old man who yells at me when I sneak through his garden and sometimes it's stray cats that live in the wild woods over here between your house and my house. What's your name?"

"Alice."

"My name is Ray, so you can call me Ray. My parents wanted a boy, but my mother couldn't have any more babies so they went ahead and named me Ray, anyway. I have a lot of code names, though. And they did finally get a boy dachshund, but I don't take him with me on patrols because he gives away my position to the enemy." Ray pulled on Sunny's long ears. "Like your dog did." Sunny wagged his tail.

"That's Sunny. Do you go to Ridge School?" asked Alice.

"Yeah, I'm in third grade. What happened to your eye?"

"I had a fight with Jimmy Breckinridge."

"Jimmy Breckinridge is my mother's second cousin's son. He's a snot."

"That's what I think, too."

"Well, do you want to play, then? You're pretty tall. You could be General MacArthur if you want to. But not with that red blouse. We'd be spotted right away. Maybe pirates. They wore red bandannas. We could board ships on the rope swing and make everybody walk the plank. But could you wear something darker tomorrow?"

"Sure," said Alice. "I hate this blouse, but my mother made it for me, so I wear it."

"My mother makes me wear all kinds of stuff. Wait till you meet her. You can't meet her today, though, because she's playing bridge. She's queen of the bridge club. That's how I escaped from the house for so long."

"She doesn't let you out of the house?"

"She's worried something terrible will happen to me. Like getting trapped in the drainpipe. Don't tell her I play there. She'll kill me. What time is it?"

"I don't know," said Alice. "Maybe about five-thirty?"

"Oh, my gosh. I have to get home. She'll have a conniption. Have you ever read *The Call of the Wild?*"

"No. Is it good?"

"It's real sad. I wasn't supposed to read it because it's too old for me, but I did, anyway, and it's great. I could bring Schnitzel tomorrow and you could bring your dog—what's his name again?—and we could play *Call of the Wild*."

"Sunny."

"But you have to read the book first."

"I will. I like to read."

"Okay, see you tomorrow. I have to go or my mother will kill me."

Ray slid through the arching branches and was gone. Alice looked after her. It was a good hideout, after all.

The Mansion

The next day, Alice hunched over her desk with her head down, partly so no one would notice her eye and partly because she was reading *The Call of the Wild* underneath her math book, and then her geography book, and then her history book. She had found *The Call of the Wild* on her father's bookshelf last night and read the first chapter under a blanket before her mother came in and took away the flashlight. She should not have brought the book to school, but it called to her.

At first she read only a page or two at a time, hurrying back to Mrs. Hopkins's assignments between pages. As the story closed in, she read more, glancing up at Mrs. Hopkins from under her hands every once in a while to pretend she was listening. Then she ran into an unexpected problem. A lot of dogs were getting killed. Dead dogs made Alice cry. She could not stop reading and she could not stop crying. It helped that generally no one paid any attention to her, but hiding from Mrs. Hopkins was hard. Alice finished a unit test on the Civil War and dove back into her book, which was well concealed under the test paper. Suddenly she became aware of a brown corduroy skirt beside her lowered head. Tears were still seeping through her eyelashes when a bony hand reached down and lifted up the paper. Mrs. Hopkins looked from the paper to the book to Alice's swollen face. Then she patted Alice's shoulder and walked on without a word. After that, Mrs. Hopkins did not call on her once. Alice finished the book and recovered in peace.

On the way to recess, she saw Ray marching off with her class to the music room. Alice walked along the hall beside her.

"Hi, Ray," said Alice.

"Hi, Ray, can I play with you and the other babies?" came a mocking voice behind them.

Ray turned around. "Shut up, Jimmy Breckinridge, or I'll tell your daddy and he'll tan your hide."

"Oh, big deal. I'm so scared."

But Alice noticed that he passed them by without saying anything else and did not bother her on the playground. She stood by the wire fence and watched the clumps of children peel off and buzz around in circles. The sky was clouding over, threatening rain. Alice tried not to think about *The Call of the Wild* because just remembering the end made her cry. After the last bell rang, she waited to collect herself and her books while the classroom emptied. On her way out, Mrs. Hopkins handed her a Kleenex.

"I don't want to pry, Alice, but one of your eyes is even more swollen than the other one. Did you have an accident?"

"Yes, ma'am."

Mrs. Hopkins waited. Alice shifted her books from one arm to the other and looked down at the floor.

"Well, if I can help in any way, let me know. And take care of yourself."

"I will."

Alice walked slowly down the hall, which was almost empty already, and through the heavy outer doors. There was Ray, chattering with three friends on the steps, her red hair flaring like a beacon against the gray sky.

"Hey, do you want to walk home together?" asked Alice.

Ray made a face. "I can't. I have car pool. My mother thinks someone will kidnap me if I walk home. Besides, it's going to rain, and she thinks I'll get sick running around in the rain." She followed Alice down the stairs. "And Alice, you'd better not talk to me in school, 'cause I'm only in third grade. They'll call you Baby. You have to pretend we're on a secret mission. That's what I do all the time. This is my disguise."

Alice looked at the yellow dress, matching yellow socks, and penny loafers that Ray's mother must have laid out for Ray to wear that morning. On Ray, it all looked like a Halloween costume.

"Okay, then, I'll see you later," said Alice.

"Right," whispered Ray, and gave Alice a quick, furtive military salute.

Alice began the long walk home. It started raining halfway there, and Jimmy Breckinridge did not appear. When Alice got to the house, her mother was doing warm-up scales.

"Change your clothes, Alice, they're soaking wet. Your father's coming home to pick you up. He's got some house calls to make." She looked up over her flying hands and then settled back down to practice.

Alice walked slowly up the stairs to her room. Ray would like Alice's room. It was a perfect lookout, but Ray's mother would never let Ray come over in the pouring rain. Alice might as well go on house calls.

She was ready when her father came, and they drove in silence for a while with only the windshield wipers swishing back and forth. It should have been cozy, but Alice felt he was far away and preoccupied.

"Do you like it here, Daddy?" she asked.

"I have to get used to it," he said. "Town life is a little cramped for my taste, but it offers a lot more for you kids."

Alice had no answer for that, and her father fell silent again.

"This patient lives on Lookout Mountain," he said finally. "It's a very ritzy area. I thought you might like to see it."

"What's wrong with her?"

"She's an alcoholic, with all the time and money she needs to drink herself sick."

"That's sad."

"Very sad. And what's sadder is that she has a teenage daughter watching her do it. Her husband took off a long time ago, and the other doctors have given up on her. That's why she first came in to see me, because I'm new in town."

The car seemed to zigzag uphill forever. Finally they got to the top of the mountain, circled into a driveway, and parked. A huge house with white columns rose before them. The mansion was ringed with carefully tended hedges and elegant autumn roses. Alice's father had never made a house call to a place like this. She felt a thorn of pain as she remembered the cabin where Leroy's mother had lived and died. Just for a second, she tasted the sweetness of fresh peach again and smelled the swampy fur of the old dog with the soft, scarred ears. What had happened to Leroy's mother's dog?

A maid in uniform greeted them at the mansion door. The hallway was tiled with marble, and the living room was entirely white, with a carpet so thick that Alice's feet sank into it. The maid motioned her to wait there and led her father away.

Alice walked over to the plate-glass windows, where a few city lights were just starting to blink far below, their colors smeared in the wet air. As she stared across the valley, she sensed something behind her and turned around. There stood a girl whose approach had been muffled in the white fleece underfoot. She had a long nose, like a troll princess, and pale eyes.

"You want to read some comic books while you wait?"

"Sure," said Alice politely.

The girl threw a pile of comic books on the glass coffee table. "Help yourself. I have the biggest collection in the world." She curled up on the spotless white sofa and sorted through the pile. "Here's a good one, *Dracula's Orgy*."

Alice looked at the cover, which showed a beautiful young woman tied down to a table, with blood draining from her throat into a golden goblet.

"Do you have any plain comic books?"

"You mean like Mickey Mouse and Donald Duck? Naw, that's baby stuff. These comic books are cool. Take a look. You'll like them. Anyway, your dad's going to be a long time. He probably has to give my old lady an intravenous solution. She won't eat when she's been on a binge."

The girl picked up a comic book called *Satan's Chamber of Horrors,* with a cover illustration devoted to instruments of torture, and immediately became engrossed in it. Alice did not want to read *Dracula's Orgy,* but she read the first page to be polite, and the second page to find out how Dracula lured the beautiful young woman to his castle, and the third page to find out what happened next. Soon she had finished the whole story and picked up another in the Dracula series.

The girl looked up from her chamber of horrors. "Cool, hunh? You can borrow one if you promise to bring it back next time your dad comes. One thing for sure, my old lady will go on another binge as soon as she gets over this one."

By the time Alice's father reappeared with his black bag, Alice was afraid to step out into the darkening evening. Somebody was sure to be lurking behind her with a long knife, or at least fangs, and she raced to keep up with her father's long strides.

"Quite a house," said her father. "Did you have fun with the daughter?"

"Sort of."

"Well, you can come with me anytime you want to. I think that girl is lonely. Her mother sure isn't much company, and you can bet your bottom dollar the maids don't stay long." The car swayed downhill into the deepening gloom of a stormy evening.

Alice's night was haunted with thunder, lightning, and dreams of being tied to a white sofa stained with blood. The next day, when her father asked if she wanted to go with him on house calls, she told him she had already promised to meet Ray.

The Ridge

Ray's mother looked Alice over very carefully. "Come on in, honey, and have some lemonade. I was just about to give Ray a little snack." Alice followed Ray's mother through the cool, dark house into a sunny kitchen, where Ray sat munching cookies from a plate piled high.

"Your guest is here, Ray."

"Hey, Alice." Ray took another cookie.

"Hay is for cows, Ray," said her mother. "Let's remember our manners. I'm sure Alice would like a cookie, too."

Ray handed Alice a sticky handful of cookies.

"The plate, honey, pass the plate. Honestly!"

Ray shoved the plate toward Alice and jumped up. "You want to see my room?"

"For goodness' sake, Ray, let her have something to eat. What does your father do, Alice?"

"He's a doctor."

"Oh, that's wonderful. My husband is a lawyer, but he has a lot of friends in the American Medical Association.

One of my bridge partners is in the AMA ladies' auxiliary club."

Alice looked down at her cookie. Her father would not join the American Medical Association because he thought the meetings were boring and the dues were high. So of course her mother did not belong to the AMA ladies' auxiliary club. Her parents did not belong to anything. In the country there had been nothing to belong to except the church and the Ku Klux Klan. Her father avoided church and despised the Ku Klux Klan.

"And what about your mother? Does she play bridge?"

"No, she plays the harp."

"Oh. How wonderful! Maybe she'll play for our garden club sometime. We have meetings every month."

"She plays for the symphony."

"Oh. Well. How wonderful."

"Mom, Alice wants to see my room."

"All right, run on, then. Alice, tell your mother I'm going to pay her a visit tomorrow. I represent the neighborhood welcome wagon. And I'll bring over a covered dish, too. I found a fabulous new recipe."

"That means she's going to make tuna noodle casserole for your supper so she can snoop around your house," whispered Ray on the way upstairs.

"She won't find much," said Alice.

"That's good," said Ray. "Then she won't come back. My mother wants my father to be a judge, see, so she has to know all the right people. They're boring, though. I don't think your family's going to fit."

Schnitzel, whose three-inch-long legs made him half the height of each stair, struggled up the steps ahead of them and into Ray's room. The first thing Alice saw, besides the pink canopy bed, was a glass cabinet with a collection of dolls from all over the world.

"Don't worry," said Ray. "We don't have to play with the dolls. They're locked up, and my mother keeps the key because they're priceless. I just have to change my clothes and then we can get out of here." Ray kicked off her loafers, trampled her dress and matching socks underfoot, pulled on a pair of brown corduroy pants, grabbed the drab green jacket, tucked her blazing hair deep under the army camouflage hat, and dragged Alice down the stairs and out the door.

"See, you want to blend in with the trees," said Ray, looking at the old gray shirt Alice had borrowed from Ben. "That's better than red, anyway."

"I read *The Call of the Wild.*"

"Did you like it?"

"Sort of. I always cry when animals get hurt."

"Gee, you must have cried all the way through."

"I did."

"Why didn't you stop reading it?"

"I had to find out what happened."

"At least the dog won."

"Yeah, but everybody else lost—the man he loved and the Indians and all those other dogs. I even felt sorry for the stupid people who fell through the ice."

"Well, it's the law of tooth and claw. Only the strongest win."

"I know."

"Anyway, my mother says I can't take Schnitzel into the woods because he'll get ticks."

"Sunny gets ticks all the time. We just pull his fur back and touch the tick's head with a burnt match. The heat makes the tick draw out and fall off. Ben squashes them, but I just flush them down the toilet."

"My mother would faint. Anyway, we should wait till wintertime to play *The Call of the Wild*, especially if it snows."

"It really snows here?"

"A little bit, if we're lucky. It doesn't stay on the ground very long, but one time they called off school."

"I've never seen snow."

"It's cold and white."

"Well, I know that."

"And there won't be any ticks. We could hitch Schnitzel and Sunny to a sled."

"Maybe," said Alice. She tried to picture Schnitzel's cigar-stub legs laboring through a snowdrift.

"Right now we could just play General MacArthur. I was in the middle of a game yesterday. See, any car that comes along the ridge of this mountain is an enemy tank. We've got to defend the ridge. You get on one side of the road, and I'll get on the other. Headquarters is the drainpipe. The first sound of anything coming, we dive into the drainpipe and take cover. Hoot like an owl to let me know you're a friendly patrol, otherwise I'll shoot. Here's a rifle."

Ray handed Alice a long stick and found another one for herself. Then she slithered into the round, gray cement tunnel and disappeared in the dark. Alice wondered if there were snakes in the drainpipe. Soon she heard a low whistle and crawled up the hill toward the road, careful to stay hidden in the thick bushes. From behind a sycamore tree, she spied a stick waving back and forth in the air. She waved her stick back and settled down to wait. It was hot and buggy, but before too long she heard the gravel-crunch of a car coming and dove down the hill, sliding part of the way on her backside and part of the way on her stomach. Before the car had gone by, they were both in the drainpipe hooting the owl signal, which echoed spookily as they crawled through the damp tunnel and met in the middle. Headquarters seemed a lot more dangerous than the battlefield.

"Do you have a handkerchief?" whispered Ray.

"No. All I've got is Kleenex."

"You'd better keep it handy in case we get captured and have to wave a white flag."

Alice pulled out a wad of Kleenex from her jeans pocket. It was still damp from yesterday's cry over *The Call of the Wild.*

"I don't think we want to use this," she said to Ray.

"Okay, tomorrow then, I'll see if I can smuggle out one of my father's handkerchiefs."

They returned to their stations alongside the ridge and encountered several more cars arriving home from work.

Suddenly, in the middle of a tunnel-crawl, they heard the faint blast of a whistle.

"Uh-oh, that's my call home, no ifs ands or buts. Do you want to play tomorrow? Oh, no, I can't play tomorrow. It's Saturday, and I have dancing lessons—ugh—and Sylvia Lattimore's birthday party—double ugh, her mother and my mother are best friends, so she and I are supposed to be best friends—and Sunday I have to go to Sunday school and church and eat dinner with all our relatives. Triple ugh. But I'll see you Monday after school. And don't forget. In school, you don't even know me. You have to protect yourself, see, because otherwise you're dead."

✣ ✣ ✣

On Saturday, Alice helped her mother do the laundry. Their machine had a ringer, and Alice had to feed wet clothes through it without getting her fingers caught. Then she hung everything up to dry in the wind. Afterward, she did her homework and watched the birds at their feeding station and thought about the dark girl, who was, Alice knew, still lonely in her canoe. On Sunday, her parents argued about whether to go to church or to go hiking.

"If the children and I go to church, Ned, we'll be back by noon and spend the afternoon with you in the woods."

"That's too late to get started, Lydia. One of my patients told me about an old trail down the side of Signal Ridge, across the valley from here, but it will take all day to hike it. We don't want to get caught on those cliffs in the dark."

"Can't we do it another time?"

"Sunday is my only day off. You know that as well as I do."

Alice was hoping her mother would hold out for church, because the Bible teacher at school kept a chart with gold stars for each Sunday that a student attended church. But her mother was already rushing to fill the picnic basket with tomatoes, cheese, bread, peaches, and lemonade. There was no time for anything else. Alice knew that if they didn't hurry, her father would leave and her mother would be tight-lipped the rest of the day and her father would not return till late enough to worry everyone. The city made him restless. Their daily walks in the Alabama woods had turned into a weekly rush for Tennessee woods as wild as her father could find.

After they were in the car and on the way, both of her

parents seemed to relax. Something wasn't right, though. Alice sat up. "Where's Sunny?" she asked.

"Didn't you bring him?" asked her mother.

"I forgot," she said miserably. "He ran out the dog door, and then Daddy started calling us and I thought . . ."

"Don't worry," said her father. "He'll be fine till we get back."

"But he loves Sunday hikes."

"Well, he's probably taking a hike of his own right now. There are a lot of rabbits in the woods by our house."

Alice looked out the window. Sunny would miss her. She already missed Sunny. They drove across the valley and started up Signal Ridge. The mountain roadsides flamed with autumn leaves, and the trail, when they started along it, seemed paved with gold. The top of Signal Ridge offered a sweeping view of the valley, all the way across to their own mountain on the other side. The air was festooned with bright reds and burnt orange. Acorns cracked underfoot, squirrels scolded above their heads. Suddenly, the trail turned down into a precarious opening through the rocky bluffs. Alice's mother stopped and looked down. "I don't know, Ned. This looks awfully steep."

"Oh, come on, Lydia, you can do it. Look at Ben. He's already halfway down the bluff."

"What about Alice?"

"What about Alice? Alice is a natural-born climber. Just pretend you're in the mimosa tree, Alice."

Somehow the mimosa seemed much safer, even though Ben finished the descent unhurt. Alice watched her father go down and then her mother, relieved when they had made it but terrified to be next.

"Do exactly what I did, Alice," called her mother from

below. "Go slowly and hang on tight. I'll be right here watching."

"What if I fall? You can't catch me."

"You're not going to fall. Just follow the way I went and you'll make it."

Alice sat and slid the first bit, then angled sideways and inched her legs down. She stretched from one rock to the next, finding handholds and footholds, slipping on bits of lichen and moss, grabbing for tough little shrubs that grew out of the cracks, hanging, finally, from the last crevice, and scraping her stomach across the stone as she dropped to solid ground.

"Whew! That was close. I don't think Sunny could have made it." She tried to stiffen her shaky knees. Why did her knees get weak when she was scared? Then she rubbed her dirt-streaked hands on her jeans and realized that her hands were shaking, too.

Her mother put an arm around her shoulder. "You did a good job, honey. That was a tall order for somebody your age. Get your breath back for just a minute, we have to catch up with Ben and your father."

Alice could see them ahead. Ben was practically swinging down the mountain from one sapling to the next, and her father was cutting a stout walking stick with his machete—the long knife that hung from his belt like a sword. When Alice and her mother came close, he held out the stick.

"Here, Lydia, this will help brace you on the climb back up."

"Thank you, Ned," said her mother stiffly.

"And congratulations, Alice, for winning the battle of the bluffs. I knew you could do it."

The rest of the trail was an easy slope, but the rough parts had taken much longer than they'd expected. Twilight closed in before they reached the bottom of the mountain and started back up. The path grew harder to see and finally disappeared in shadows. For a few minutes, Ben thought he had found it again, but the clearing he followed soon narrowed to an animal trail that angled off across the mountainside into thick brush.

"This is impossible, Ned. We can't risk going up those cliffs in the dark."

"We'll just have to sleep here, Lydia. Ben and I will cut some branches for bedding while you and Alice make a fire."

"With what?"

"Didn't you bring any matches?"

"I didn't have time. You were in such a hurry to get going. And we weren't planning to cook out."

"Well, the temperature's going to drop, but at least it's not raining." Alice's father drew the machete from his belt and began hacking at branches. Ben piled them into a platform, and Alice threw leaves on top. It was fun, in a way, the first thing they had done together for ages. By the time they all buried themselves in leaves, the mountain was thickly spread with cold, black silence.

"What about school tomorrow?" whispered Alice.

"We'll cross that bridge in the morning," said her mother grimly. "Let's just get through the night first."

"Do you think Sunny's okay?"

"Sunny's probably a lot better off than we are right now. He's got food, water, and the dog door if he wants to go in or out."

Between the prickly branches underneath and the

scratchy leaves on top, Alice lay listening to occasional rustling from some animal visitor. Thank goodness there were no leopards in east Tennessee. Unless one escaped from the zoo. There was always that possibility. A leopard *could* be hiding on the mountain. She looked over at her father. He was breathing deeply and seemed to have gone sound asleep. She wondered if her mother was sleeping. She knew Ben wasn't, because he tossed and turned, scrunching the leaves with every move.

"What's wrong, Ben?" her mother finally asked.

"I have to go to the bathroom."

"Go on, then, and settle down so we can sleep a little."

Ben scuttled out from the pile of leaves and walked off a little way into the dark. Alice heard a scuffling noise and then a dry rattling that did not sound like leaves.

"Mother, did you hear that?" said Ben, in a tiny strangled voice.

"Yes, son, don't move."

Ben stood there a long time till the rattling stopped and there was a slight rustling that did sound like leaves, like something gliding away through dry leaves. Still, Ben stood, until finally Alice's mother said, "Now move back slowly."

Finally, Ben crawled into their makeshift bed. He was shaking, not just his hands or his knees, but all over his body. When Alice reached over, he pulled away.

"Was it a rattlesnake?" she whispered.

"I don't know, Alice, but everything's fine now, so don't worry about it," answered her mother. Ben said nothing.

When bits of daybreak began to sift through the trees, Alice rolled stiffly off the piled branches. Her mother and

Ben looked pale and puffy-eyed, exactly like Alice felt. Her father looked fine. In the gray light, he found the path, and they hauled themselves toward the bluffs. Although she dreaded the ascent, climbing up seemed easier than climbing down, maybe because facing upward kept her from seeing the ground below, maybe because Alice felt numb as a robot. She climbed and walked automatically. Nobody spoke. Nobody mentioned the rattling sound in the middle of the night. By the time they reached the car, waiting patiently on top of Signal Ridge, a metallic sun was heating up the day.

"Say, I think you kids can still make it to school," said Alice's father gaily. He drove home singing "Oh, What a Beautiful Morning," his favorite song from *Oklahoma!*, at the top of his lungs. He ruffled Sunny's ears when Sunny came charging wildly out the dog door to greet them. He complimented Alice's mother on her coffee. He waved as Ben glowered out the door. He gave Alice a lift to school, with Sunny riding between them in the front seat of the car. She had not seen her father this happy since the move.

Alice, on the other hand, felt very tired, with a headache fuzzing her eyes. During spelling, she discovered that she had forgotten to brush her hair. Leaf bits fell from her braids all day long, and when the Bible teacher came for the weekly Monday visit, Alice's row on the Church Chart showed another empty space between the gold stars above and the gold stars below.

The Playground

Mrs. Hopkins swept the room with her eyes and fixed on Jimmy Breckinridge, who had turned around to poke Dick Burkhart with a folded note. "Jimmy, tell us what you learned last night from reading the history assignment about the post–Civil War period."

Jimmy slid down in his seat and mumbled.

"What's that, Jimmy? I couldn't hear you."

"Nothing."

"You said nothing, or you learned nothing?"

"I said I don't see why we have to read about stuff that happened a hundred years ago."

"Because it affects what's happening today, Jimmy, that's why. If you look at the newspaper, you'll find some of the same issues are still causing a lot of trouble."

"Like what?"

"Segregation, for one thing. The laws that were passed in the South after the Civil War created a new kind of racial separation that has finally been challenged in the Supreme Court. The court's decision last year, that separate schools are not equal schools, will affect all of us."

"Not me," said Jimmy. "My daddy says that if we have to integrate here, he'll just send me to a private school."

"But in a democracy, Jimmy, don't you think that every person should have an equal chance? How about the rest of you? Surely you wouldn't all leave Ridge School. How many of you would stay here and welcome the newcomers to this school?"

"You mean Negroes?" asked Mary Jane McCall.

"Yes, racial equality is the issue here."

"You mean in class here? You mean sit by them?" Mary Jane McCall sat on her hands.

Alice looked around the room. No one was raising a hand. Alice did not want to raise her hand. She knew if she did it would make everything worse. She knew it was going to make everything worse. Slowly her arm rose into the air, wavered for a moment, and straightened, as if it had a life of its own, as if it remembered Leroy's arm raised high in the hot sun on the chicken coop roof, bang, bang, bang, bang. Alice's arm waved to Leroy, somewhere else in the world. The rest of her body waited below, disconnected, watching what would happen next. First there was silence, while everyone stared at her. Then there was clamor, as everyone talked at once. Alice's head pounded, bang, bang, bang, bang.

Mrs. Hopkins stood for a moment, looking around the room. Then she walked over to the side wall and flicked off the light switch. Suddenly it was much darker in the room, and quieter.

"Whatever your opinion, there's no reason to lose control of yourselves," she said softly. "In the future, please remember that principle. It's the basis for a democracy, and it's the basis for discussions in this classroom. There appears to be a clear majority for segregation here, but some of you may want to keep an open mind and think about it further. I strongly recommend that you gather as much information as you can, not only from your parents, but also from newspaper and magazine articles by people who may disagree with your parents. If you would be interested in writing on this issue, you may do so for extra credit. We are going to get back to work now. Please open your math books to the exercise at the end of Chapter Five. Pass your papers to the front of the room when the bell rings for recess."

Alice stared at the math book in front of her. The numbers and words seemed like a foreign language that, try as she might, she could not translate. Finally, she abandoned the math book and looked out the window, thinking about Leroy. Then her mind slid away from Leroy to the dark girl. She could see the dark girl more clearly in her mind now than she could in the picture above Mrs. Hopkins's desk. When the bell rang, she knew that the dark girl was not only alone, she was also surrounded by enemies. She had to paddle her canoe very quietly, stay hidden, and never steer too close to the banks of the stream.

When Alice walked toward the door, the others left a wide space around her. But out on the playground they formed two lines on either side of her, shouting, "ABE LINCOLN, ABE LINCOLN, ABE LINCOLN." Alice broke through the line on one side and ran toward a playground monitor.

"I have to go to the bathroom," she panted.

"Can't you wait till recess is over?"

"No, I really have to go."

The playground monitor sighed and looked at her watch. "Oh, all right," she said. "Go on in. But you're going to miss out on the game over there, and it looks like fun."

Alice turned to see what the playground monitor was looking at. The two lines had merged into one, all facing her and shouting as loud as they could, "ABE LINCOLN, ABE LINCOLN, ABE LINCOLN." She raced into the building toward the bathroom, lowered her pulsing head over the toilet, and threw up.

✥ ✥ ✥

"I'm proud of you," said Alice's mother. "You stood up for what you believed was right. That's a hard thing to do."

✥ ✥ ✥

"I can't play with you anymore," said Ray. "I had to come on a special mission to tell you."

"Why not? Why can't you play with me?"

"Because Jimmy Breckinridge's mother called my mother and said there was some kind of trouble at school about segregation, and my mother says that if there's going to be trouble at school she doesn't want me mixed up with it or with anyone who's involved in it."

"That's not fair. I didn't make any trouble at school."

"I told her that, but she said trouble is trouble no matter who makes it, just stay away from it."

"We can't play ever again, or just now?"

"Well, we could pretend that the wild stretch between our houses is enemy territory and that we couldn't go there without getting blown up."

"That's not really playing."

"I can't help it, Alice, she's my mother and I have to do what she says."

"What if what she says isn't right?"

Ray's hazel eyes suddenly watered and turned red. "I don't know," she cried.

Alice watched her turn away—coppery hair uncoiling from the camouflage cap—and retreat blindly through the bushes of enemy territory.

The Ship

A cold wind bared the trees that had hidden Alice's house from Ray's. There was no snow, but brown leaves covered the ground. Alice heaped them into hills, took running jumps, and flew crashing into the piles, with Sunny tumbling behind her. She spied several of the stray cats that had claimed that strip of wilderness for their own, but they streaked away in fear as soon as they saw her. It was hard to sneak through the woods without leafy branches and bushes to hide behind. It was also not very interesting when there was no one to hide with. Alice spent hours swinging on the rope and, after a rainy weekend reading *Treasure Island,* made a series of treasure maps that she tore around the edges and rubbed in the dirt for an antique effect. Since Ray had not reappeared, she tried to enlist Ben in her crew.

"You could be first mate," she pleaded, looking at the tools neatly hung from a Peg-Board over his worktable.

"I'm too old to play pirates."

"You could be captain, even."

"You're too old to play pirates, too, Alice. Why don't you call up some of your friends?"

"I don't have any."

"Oh, come on, Alice."

In the far corner of Ben's room, Alice could see his old saddle gathering dust on the back of a chair. "Would you take me riding sometime?" she asked.

"Where?" he asked.

"There's a stable on Signal Ridge. I saw the sign."

"Ask Daddy to take you."

"Remember that time you fell off Lucky Jim? And you had to walk on crutches? They're in the basement, and you could use one of them to be Long John Silver. He has a peg leg. Have you ever read *Treasure Island*?"

Ben turned away. "I've got homework, Alice."

When Alice went downstairs, her father was listening intently to the news. She waited for the advertisements, when he always lowered the volume.

"Did you hear that, Alice? Martin Luther King's leading a bus boycott in Montgomery. That'll hit bigots where it hurts, right in the pocketbook!"

"Do you think Leroy knows about it?"

"You can bet your sweet life Leroy knows about it. Everybody knows about it. That's why it might work."

"Do you think we'll ever see Leroy again?"

"I doubt it."

Alice fell silent. She looked out the window at the blue mountain ridges rising on the horizon as far as she could see. Somewhere beyond them was Leroy, walking, riding, flying East of the Sun and West of the Moon, to live south of the sun and moon no more. "Do you think we'll ever go back to Alabama?"

"We'll probably visit your grandparents next summer."

"No, I mean to live."

"No, not to live."

Not to live, not to live, what a ghostly feeling. . . . Alabama was gone from her, like a lost world. Even though she went back to visit, it was never going to be the same as living there. Alabama felt like an empty space on the map because she wasn't in it anymore. Her grandparents were there, but even her grandparents seemed unreal. They had disappeared except for a few formal words on the telephone. "Hello, Alice." "Hello, Grandmother, how are you?" They might as well be in India, a place she knew only from stories. In a way, now, Alabama seemed like a place she knew only from stories—Alice and the swimming pool, Alice and the alligator pond, Alice and the bamboo nest. None of those places existed in the same way without her. They were vacant, like the pasture without Lucky Jim. But something even stranger—the pasture with Lucky Jim in it, which was just a story in her head now, seemed more real than the pasture without Lucky Jim, the way it really was now.

"Could we go horseback riding here sometime? You said you'd teach me how to ride."

"When did I say that?"

"Before we left Alabama."

"Oh. Sure, we'll have to find a stable."

"There's one on Signal Ridge. I saw the sign."

"All right. Be quiet now, Alice, the news is coming back on."

Alice went outside to swing aboard imaginary ships on the long, strong rope, out over the terrace and back, out and back. How could Ben be too old to play? How could anybody? The girls at school pretended to be grown up, but they were really just playing. The lipstick and powder they put in their purses and spread out on the bathroom sink seemed like toys. Playing with each other's hair was like a game of beauty parlor. It was a really boring game, but at least it was a game. Ben never played anything. Mostly now he did homework and made things with tools, fancy carved wooden things like jewelry boxes and breadboards and corner shelves. If Alice touched his tools, he yelled at her, so she tried to stay out of his room.

The day after Alice asked him to play pirates, Ben put up a sign on his door saying, KEEP OUT and started a maddening racket of hammering and sawing.

"Sounds like Ben's starting a construction company," said Alice's father. Then he turned away and winked at Alice's mother in a secret way.

"Go call him for dinner, Alice," she said, "but knock before you enter, don't just barge in."

"I never do that!" said Alice. "I mean, barge in. I always knock! Why does he have to be so private all the time, anyway? I don't put up any big KEEP OUT signs on my door."

"It's just a phase, Alice. He's an adolescent. He'll grow out of it . . . and you'll grow into it."

Never, thought Alice. She would have a big sign on her door saying, COME IN.

As Christmas vacation got closer, Ben kept up the noise every day after school, but there would be long periods of silence between hammering and sawing and drilling. The silence was even more maddening than the noise. The noise told Alice that something was definitely going on; the silence made her wonder what.

Alice did not make any Christmas presents. Instead,

her mother took her shopping downtown, where they rode up and down escalators looking over peoples' heads toward Christmas trees that towered to the ceilings of the sparkling stores. Their own tree came from the woods, as usual, dug up from a crowded stand of cedars and named Jade. Jade was going to start a new grove in their terraced yard. Still, the season seemed strangely changed. Alice felt homesick. Christmas made the old sights and sounds of Alabama seem farther away than ever. From this distance, though, she could see something new. Each person's Alabama was different, Leroy's from hers, for instance. *You just think what it would be like to live in a big white cage all the time, honey.* What was Leroy doing this Christmas without Alabama? *It's a funny thing—he's traveling, now, but he's home free, home free.* What were Myrtle and Zelda doing right now? Did they all miss her? What were her grandmother and grandfather doing? Well . . . some things stayed the same. Her grandfather was smoking his cigar, and her grandmother was making tea, and Pixie was yapping at nothing. It was a funny thing, though, she missed her grandparents. Curry dinners were not the same without chapatis. She even missed Ben, for goodness' sake, and he was right downstairs in his room.

"But I have you, Sunny," she whispered into his long, soft ears at night. "You are one year old, and that is not too old to play and we are going to play forever." *Old Man Forever can fool you. . . .* One thing for sure, Leroy was going to stay in her head, wherever else he was. And he was going to keep talking to her, whatever else he was doing.

✣ ✣ ✣

On Christmas morning, Alice heard what sounded like a shot in the side yard. Before she could even get out of bed, Ben rushed in with a white handkerchief and tied it around her eyes.

"Better come with me, mate," he growled. "Here, put your coat on over your pajamas."

"I can't see anything."

"You don't need to see anything."

Alice could hear her parents whispering behind them as she was half pulled, half prodded along with a sharp object. She could tell by the direction they walked and the feel of the ground that Ben was leading her toward the old oak tree. When he jerked the blindfold from her face, Alice saw, on the terrace below her rope swing, the perfect replica of a pirate ship.

"Oh, look!" she cried.

The ship itself was outlined by boards painted black and shaped like a low hull, with the ground inside serving as deck. Sticking up in the middle was a mast with bed-sheet sails that could be lowered and raised through a system of pulleys and clothesline. At the top of the mast flew a black flag, skull and crossbones sewn in white and rippling in the wintry wind. A wooden cannon was painted gold and mounted on a block with wheels so it could be swiveled back and forth, depending on the direction from which enemies attacked. Against the cannon leaned a handsome wooden cutlass with coconut-shell hand guards. Ben stood proudly at the helm, which not only turned, but was also attached to a rudder that moved back and forth. The crowning touch was a hinged chest spilling out treasures of dime store jewelry and gold-foiled chocolate coins.

For a long time, Alice could only stare at Ben's creation.

"Come on, don't you want to fire the cannon?" he asked.

Then she was grabbing the rope with a shriek and soaring out over the terrace to drop neatly aboard.

"See, it fires with caps." Ben snapped a hammer device down on a red cap, which made the loud pop Alice had heard. It smelled sulfurous and smoked gallantly. Alice's parents smiled down at them while Ben showed her all the hidden features of the pirate ship, giving instructions on how to work things so she wouldn't break his cunning inventions. When he had finished his grand tour, Alice sat down on the treasure chest.

"Watch it!" he exclaimed. "That's not an easy chair."

"Oh, Ben. Thank you. It's like a fairy-tale ship."

"Fairy tales don't have pirates in them, Dumbo."

"Well, a story ship, then. I love it. I can hardly believe it, everything looks so real."

"It is real. I made it," said Ben smugly.

"I mean, you know, like a real-life ship that sails away on the water."

"Well, I couldn't manage the water. You have to imagine that, and also the pirates—I dub thee captain, first mate, and crew." With a flourish, he handed her two black eye patches.

"Hey, one for me and one for you," said Alice.

"Well, one for you and one for Ray," said Ben.

Alice said nothing.

"I was going to let you smash a bottle on the hull to launch it, but Mother wouldn't let me. She didn't want to cope with any more cut hands. Come on, let's fire the cannon again. I've got a lot of caps."

Firing the cannon was clearly Ben's favorite part. Alice wondered if he would consent to be the gunner.

"Hey, you two," called her father, "before you embark on the maiden voyage, I have a present for the family, too, a little different from Ben's, but along the same lines."

"What on earth, Ned?" asked Alice's mother. Alice's father didn't usually do much in the way of presents. Her mother said it was because he didn't get many when he was growing up. He spent birthdays at boarding school and Christmas in church.

Alice's father led the family around the back of the house where they kept the lawn mower and garden tools. There they saw a long object resting on sawhorses and covered with a huge square of canvas. Alice's father pulled off the canvas with a flourish, as if unveiling a statue. Underneath was a dark green, fiberglass canoe.

"I got this secondhand from a patient," he said. "Now we can explore the islands in Lake Chickamauga."

"But, Ned, you know I can't swim!" said Alice's mother.

"You'll wear a life jacket," said Alice's father impatiently. "Besides, if you fall in, we'll rescue you." He grinned at Ben, who ran his hand over the canoe.

"Nice lines," said Ben. "It'll carry all four of us and enough gear to camp out."

"Can Sunny go, too?" asked Alice.

"Sure. Sunny swims better than anybody."

"It's awfully cold this time of year to spend much time on the lake," said Alice's mother.

"They say that winter is the best time to look for arrowheads. The lake is lower in the winter, with a lot of exposed shore where the Cherokee Indians used to live. We can have a treasure hunt, right, Alice?"

"Sure!" Alice shouted at her father. "And thanks, Daddy, for getting us the canoe." She was already running back to swing out over her pirate ship. Sunny agreed to be second mate, although he declined to wear his black eye patch, and Alice practiced giving him orders until her mother forced her inside for breakfast. Afterward, she spent an hour putting the sail up and down, steering the rudder, swinging the cutlass, firing the cannon, and counting the treasure. Then, suddenly, she had nothing else to do. All the important parts of the game that had taken all day—digging lines in the dirt to make an imaginary ship, finding the right sticks to serve as swords, digging up rocks for treasure—didn't need to be done anymore. Alice's oceans of adventure seemed to dry up.

Well, at least the ship would never sink. It was a wonderful ship. Ben was wonderful to make it. She put the cutlass on top of the cannon so the second mate wouldn't chew on it. Then she wandered over to her hideout and settled down with Sunny to spy on invading cars and pedestrian infiltrators who might venture along the road on Christmas day. Ray would have liked the pirate ship, she thought.

The Island

The canoe was a lot more crowded than the pirate ship, and the wind, as Alice's mother had predicted, was cold. Alice huddled inside her life jacket while her father and Ben paddled them all across the choppy lake. The island they were aiming to explore was heavily wooded, the shore sloping from large rocks to a pebbly beach. They circled to find a sandy stretch and landed the canoe. As soon as they got out, Sunny found a stick and dropped it on Alice's foot, begging her to throw it into the water. When Alice tried to walk ahead, Sunny picked up the stick and dropped it on her foot again. Finally Alice threw it. In spite of the cold, Sunny swam out, grabbed the stick, swam back, shook water all over Alice's jeans, and dropped the stick on her foot again. Alice's father joined the game and threw the stick farther. Sunny retrieved every stick earnestly, as if it were a duck for dinner. After unloading the picnic gear, they all walked slowly along the shore, studying the sand and rock for chips of flint.

"I got one!" shouted Ben. Alice ran over and saw in

Ben's curled fingers an arrowhead with only one triangular corner broken off. She looked at it jealously, determined to find her own. Each new curve of the shoreline had a promising patch of chipped flint that lured her on, just a little farther, just a little farther. Any minute now she was going to find, flat and perfect on the gritty ground, an arrowhead or speartip or axhead. This was a real Treasure Island.

At last her father called her back to help start a fire and cook the hamburgers they'd brought. For once, no one had forgotten the matches or the salt or the rolls, and they ate their meal in the peaceful space between lapping waves and crackling flames.

"We need to get started back soon, Ned. Those storm clouds are building up."

"We'll be fine, Lydia. Our canoe is sturdier than it looks. I'd like to scout around a little longer."

"You scout around, then, while I clean up and get ready to go. Ben, stay and help me, please. Alice made the hamburgers."

"Ha-ha," said Alice.

"Buzz off, rat fink," said Ben.

Alice and her father tramped through a stand of scrubby pines, with Sunny rushing ahead in the underbrush. They heard him barking long before they saw the water moccassin, mud-colored, cottonmouthed. Sunny circled it, barking and barking, darting back and forth, back and forth.

"Sunny!" screamed Alice.

As she turned to her father, she heard him, unbelievably, call, "Sic 'im, boy!"

"No! No! No!" Alice screamed again. She ran toward Sunny to grab his collar and pull him off. Suddenly, her father was beside her with his forked walking stick. He brought it down from his great height onto the snake's neck in a lightning stroke. Seizing the snake's thrashing tail, he released the stick and cracked the long body like a whip. The snake hung broken-spined, jerking limply from his hand.

Alice scooped up her panting dog. "He could have been killed," she shouted. "He could have been killed like Lucky Jim."

"No," said her father, tossing the snake back into the bushes. "It was sluggish from the cold, probably hibernating. Didn't you see? It wasn't even coiled up to strike."

Alice turned and ran back toward the shore. She pushed the canoe into shallow water, crawled in, and held Sunny in her lap, where he licked the salty tears from her face. She could feel the faraway tap of a headache coming on.

"Are you set to go already, Alice?" called her mother.

"You're going to drift away," said Ben as he loaded the cooking gear. He helped Alice's mother tie on her fat orange life jacket and settle cautiously into the middle seat. Then he climbed into the back and turned the canoe toward Alice's father, who was wading toward them.

"I'll steer this time," said Ben.

"Fine, son," said Alice's father, and he stepped delicately, like a heron, from the deepening water into the front of the canoe. Alice watched from behind as he lifted and dipped, lifted and dipped, trailing only a few drops of water with each reach of his long arms.

After Christmas vacation, Mrs. Hopkins started weekly spelling bees. The class was divided into two teams, and the winners from each team got to captain the next week's teams. There wasn't any room for guesswork. The rules included defining the words, as well as spelling them right and then using them in a sentence.

"Language is like the stars," said Mrs. Hopkins. "If you learn a new word every day of your lives, you can explore the galaxy."

"If you lived to be seventy, you'd know 25,550 words," said Mary Jane McCall.

"Good math, Mary Jane, but still not enough words to say everything you think and feel in a lifetime. You and Alice are captains again this week."

For the first time since she had started school, Alice was leader of a team, not just once, but six weeks in a row—she and Mary Jane McCall. Mary Jane was a slightly better speller because she memorized word lists. Alice was slightly better at defining and using the words, because she read more. Their teams were even, three wins each. Every time Alice was the last to sit down, Jimmy Breckinridge snickered "Queen Bee" not quite loud enough for Mrs. Hopkins to hear. But Alice liked winning, anyway. *Go on, Queen Bee, I'm listening.*

The two captains always selected the best spellers first—otherwise there was no hope of winning. That left the unpredictable spellers and the bad spellers. Of these, Mary Jane picked her friends first, and Alice took the left-overs. Jimmy Breckinridge was always last to be selected and first to miss a word. Still, Mary Jane usually picked him because there was a new girl named Frances, a bad speller whom Mary Jane disliked even more than she did Jimmy Breckinridge.

"My mother says she's Italian and Catholic and has

nine brothers and sisters," said Mary Jane to Sue Lacey while they were combing their hair in the bathroom.

Alice wanted to make friends with Frances, but Frances kept to herself in class and always had company on the playground. During Frances's first day of recess, when Jimmy Breckinridge yelled "Frances's pants-is coming down," he was surprised to find himself suddenly facing two Franceses. Frances had a twin sister in the other fifth-grade class, and outside the classroom the two stuck together every minute. Alice would have liked to have had a twin sister, too, like the dark girl who lived in her head.

The dark girl kept her company on Valentine's Day, when Alice received exactly two Valentines, one from Jimmy Breckinridge—which said, "Roses are red, Violets are blue, Lemons are sour, And so are you"—and one from Mary Jane McCall, whose mother made her send the same kind of Valentine card to every single person in order to set a democratic example for the classroom. Mrs. McCall took her role as class mother seriously. She wore an apron with red hearts on it. She passed out cupcakes, ginger ale, and handfuls of game cards to everyone.

"This is a game," said Mrs. McCall, holding up one of the cards, "where you list as many words as you can that begin with the letters in Valentine's Day. Any questions? Yes, Mary Jane?"

"Can we use the same letters more than once, and can we use proper names, and can we use all the cards we want?"

"Of course, dear, the point is to figure out a lot of words, to fill up as many cards as you can—but those are good questions. Any more? Jimmy?"

"How come we have to use cards?"

"Well, Jimmy, that way everybody starts with the same blank materials."

"You mean, so we don't cheat? Like we might have little lists of words in our back pocket?"

"Are there any more questions? Yes, Jimmy?"

"When can we go home?"

"After the party, Jimmy, it's a regular school day. All right, class, we're timing you, so don't start till I say, 'Go.'"

Alice looked at her two Valentine cards and the heaps of Valentine cards on the desks around her and decided not to play the game. She always lost games. The rest of the class chewed their sticky cupcakes and licked their fingers and watched Mrs. McCall.

"Ready . . . ?" Mrs. McCall's red dress quivered. "Set . . . ?" She rose on tiptoe in her red shoes. "GO!"

While the others started scribbling wildly on their cards, Alice sat still and looked around the room. She noticed that Jimmy had hung a little blue and gray Dixie flag on the side of his desk. She stared out the window. She practiced drumming her fingers without making any noise. Soon Mrs. McCall walked over to her desk and leaned down.

"Look, dear," she whispered, "you just make as many words as you can starting with the letters in *Valentine's Day*. Doesn't that sound like fun? But you have to get started. It's a contest. Part of your time is already gone."

Without being rude, Alice couldn't disregard Mrs. McCall. Slowly she picked up her pencil and began writing down words. *Veranda, alligator, leopard, eggs, nest, trees, India, never, east, snake, dark, Alabama, yap.* It was too easy. There were *myriad* words starting with the letters in Valentine's Day, though *myriad* wasn't one of them. She wrote faster. Turning letters into words was like doing a puzzle, like turning thoughts into words. She liked this kind of puzzle. She could play words forever. She had a secret section in the back of her notebook just for turning thoughts into words, her own thoughts into her own words. Alice wrote more words, picked up speed, grabbed more cards, wrote more words. She was completely lost in the Valentine's Day game when Mrs. McCall called time and collected the cards. She sat back, dizzy with words. There was a flurry of counting while everyone dabbled with the gluey cupcake crumbs, and then came the announcement.

"Our winner is Alice Ryder."

Alice could hardly believe her own name. She sat still and waited in case there was a mistake. No one else got up.

"Alice? Alice Ryder?"

Finally Alice maneuvered herself from behind the wooden desk, with its chair too closely attached, and went to the front of the room. Fifty restive eyes—one pair crossed above a stuck-out tongue—followed her to the front of the room.

"Jimmy, please restore your face to its normal condition," said Mrs. McCall. "And congratulations, Alice, there's a fabulous prize for this game." Mrs. McCall handed Alice a thin package nearly as tall as she was. Inside the brown paper wrapping was a pair of red stilts.

"Just what she needs," said Jimmy Breckinridge. "Now she'll be tall as the Empire State Building."

Alice's face turned as red as the stilts. Her heart pulsed, pounded, and hammered, all three at once. She was embarrassed, she was happy. Jubilant. Triumphant. Synonyms flashed through her mind like a thesaurus. She marched back down the aisle, sat down, and held the red stilts upright beside her. Even resting on the floor, they rose above her head like two exclamation points, like two arms waving high in the air.

"All right, class, time to clean up. Let's see who can finish first."

There was an instant screaking of desk chairs, crackling of papers, thudding of books, jabbering of voices, and popping of loafers and sneakers as they came unstuck from bits of cake and icing. When the bell rang, twenty-three children hurtled toward the door. Mrs. McCall looked vastly relieved. Mary Jane stayed at her desk primly organizing her homework assignments while her mother gathered her wits and her possessions.

Alice carried the stilts out of the classroom on her shoulder and did not flinch when Ray saw her and turned away in the hall. She practiced the stilts on the way home and felt elevated with pride. It was the high point of the year so far.

The Classroom

When the Bible teacher came into the room, Mrs. Hopkins always left. Then the noise level went up. The noise level went up partly because all the students had to take turns reciting the Bible verses they had selected for the week, and partly because Miss Pilsen could not control the class.

"Now, boys and girls, let's not get out of hand."

"Let's not get out of hand" was Miss Pilsen's favorite expression, and she said it so desperately that Alice felt sorry for her, almost. Almost, but not quite, because Miss Pilsen always called on Alice first, since Alice never talked to anyone or passed notes or launched paper airplanes or threw spitballs. Miss Pilsen seemed to think that being first to recite Bible verses was Alice's reward for not getting out of hand.

"Alice, what did you memorize this week?"

"Psalm 121."

"Would you like to share it with us?"

No, thought Alice. But she did not get out of hand.

Backtalking still tasted like soap. Alice stood up and raised her voice slightly over the buzzing classroom.

> "'I will lift up my eyes unto the hills, from whence cometh my help. My help cometh from the Lord, which made heaven and earth. He will not suffer thy foot to be moved. He that keepeth thee will not slumber. Behold, he that keepeth Israel shall neither slumber nor sleep. The Lord is thy keeper. The Lord is thy shade upon thy right hand. The sun shall not smite thee by day nor the moon by night.'"

Alice paused. Leroy's voice came to her like a deep green wind. *The sun shall not smite thee by day nor the moon by night. See how much you learned from your grandmama?* Alice had to admit that Grandmother had been a help in the Bible verse department.

"Go on, Alice," urged Miss Pilsen. "You're doing very well."

Alice stared past Miss Pilsen as if she weren't there and finished the verse.

> "'The Lord shall preserve thee from all evil. He shall preserve thy soul. The Lord shall preserve thy going out and thy coming in from this time forth and even forevermore.'"

"Very nice, Alice. Now then, Sue Lacey, what did you learn this week?" Sue Lacey had learned the shortest verse in the Bible. She stood up very straight and said, "'Jesus wept.' John 11:35."

After everyone else had recited, it was time for gold stars. Alice dreaded the moment when Miss Pilsen passed around the box of gold stars. Each student who had attended church the past Sunday licked the back of a star and stuck it on the attendance chart. Between the long rows of gold stars, Alice's row had mostly blank spaces. She wondered sometimes how Miss Pilsen could tell if a person really went to church. Did she call up and check? It would be so easy, even if Alice's father had dragged them off to explore a new canyon somewhere, to stick on a gold star. But that would be a lie, and lying made Alice nervous. For one thing, it was wrong. For another thing, it would be terrible to get caught. Lying reminded Alice of wasp stings and the fires of Hell.

There was a lot of coming and going as students left their seats, stuck on their stars, and returned to sit down. As usual, Alice stayed put. Miss Pilsen beckoned her to the front desk.

"Alice, dear," said Miss Pilsen.

I am not your dear, thought Alice. "Yes, ma'am?" she said politely.

"Are you by any chance Jewish?"

"No, ma'am."

"Well, I can't help noticing how often you don't go to church. Do you perhaps go to Sunday school? That would count, too, you know."

"No ma'am, most of the time I don't go to either one."

"Well, I'd love to talk to your mother about this sometime. You're doing a good job of memorizing the Bible verses, but I'm afraid your church attendance record is going to lower the whole class average. I'm going to give you a note to take home."

"Yes, ma'am." Alice took the note back to her seat and put it with her homework assignments. Later that afternoon, she dutifully gave it to her mother.

"How dare she?" said Alice's mother. "Yes, I will certainly be glad to meet with Miss Pilsen."

"What are you going to tell her?"

"That we are often occupied on Sunday mornings hiking with your father and that it is no fault of yours and no business of anyone else's."

"What if she gets mad?"

"I don't care if she does."

"I do."

"Alice, religion is a personal matter. You can worship in a pine woods if you want to."

"But we don't."

"We experience the beauty of creation with thankful hearts. If that's not worship, I don't know what is."

"Well, just don't get her mad at me."

"I will make sure that if she's mad at anyone, Alice, it will be at me."

Alice went slowly outdoors to walk on her stilts and swing on her rope, with Sunny commanding the pirate ship below.

"Alice, if you could stay after school for a few minutes, I'd like a chance to talk to you," said Mrs. Hopkins.

Alice stopped piling her books together for the walk home and sat very still to ease the headache that visited her every afternoon. The bad ones made her eyes blur, and any quick movement made her feel like throwing up. She did not want to talk to Mrs. Hopkins or anybody else. The room emptied slowly while Alice sat and waited, her head banging like pounded nails, bang, bang, bang, bang. What did Mrs. Hopkins want?

When everyone had gone, Mrs. Hopkins got up, closed the door, and walked over to sit down. She fit much more neatly into the school desk than Alice did.

"I've had a chat with Miss Pilsen and also with your mother, who came in yesterday to discuss the Church Chart problem."

Alice nodded her head.

"I'm aware, Alice, that this has not been an easy year for you."

Alice nodded her head again, her eyes blurred and watering. She would not cry and she would not throw up.

"I'm also aware that you do a lot of reading, and your classwork shows a gift for words. However, when I've provided opportunites for creative writing, you have not turned anything in. I realize that writing can be a very private act, but your mother did mention to me that she thought you were doing some writing. I want you to know that I'd like to see your work if you feel like showing it to me, and that whatever you show me would be strictly confidential. Sometimes a person can say things in writing that she can't say out loud."

Alice nodded once more, because she could think of nothing to say out loud. And really, she had nothing to say in private. The dark girl lived in her head, painful as it was just now, and seemed to be part of a story that would someday tell itself but was not ready yet. All she saw were images of the canoe going through dangerous waters, of the fear and loneliness the dark girl suffered. What made the journey necessary and the loneliness fearful was not clear.

Mrs. Hopkins seemed to be waiting for something. Alice knew from experience that Mrs. Hopkins could practice silence for a long time if she was waiting for something—for people to answer questions, for instance.

"I did write something after we talked about segregation, but it's not what you asked us to do."

"What do you mean?"

"I didn't read the newspapers or talk to anybody or anything. It's just some thoughts."

"Would you mind letting me read it?"

"You won't show it to anybody?"

"Not without your permission."

Alice slowly shuffled through her notebook, snapped open the three-ring binder, and lifted out the last page.

Mrs. Hopkins took the piece of paper and looked at it for a long time.

"This is a poem, Alice, and quite an expressive one. Poetry is a different kind of knowledge, but just as important as any facts you might organize for a report. This is very promising. I would encourage you to write more and, whenever you want, to show it to me. I could help you work on revisions that will make your writing even better."

Alice felt little stars explode in her head. She looked at the paper Mrs. Hopkins handed back.

White hates black;
black hates white;
blue hates gray;
gray hates blue;
they jeer and call
each other yellow;
and when emotion

melts their reason,
smear green fields with red.

O Lord, sometimes
I wonder why
you did not mix
your colors,
and make us all
a faded nondescript.

The first part had come with a rush—the colors of segregation, the colors of the Civil War, the color of fear, the color of pain. The last part had been hard. She had found the word *nondescript* in *Roget's Thesaurus*, as a synonym for *colorless*, and looked it up in the dictionary: "so lacking in recognizable character or qualities as to belong to no definite class or type; hard to classify or describe; a nondescript person or thing." And the sound of *script* echoed the sound of *mix*, even though it didn't rhyme exactly. Alice had been consumed with fitting the words together, but when she looked at them the next day, they seemed stupid. She had almost thrown the final copy into the wastebasket, along with the pages and pages of scribbled work sheets—so many pages for so few words.

"You'd better start home soon, Alice. Thank you for staying late. And don't worry about your Church Chart. I don't think Miss Pilsen will mention it again. As your mother said, there are many alternatives to worshiping in church. One of them is worshiping in words. Fine writing is an act of faith."

The Hotel

"What are you making?" asked Alice, jumping down from her stilts.

"A cat trap," said her father.

"How come?"

"Our house is right on a bird migration path, and the spring migrations have started. Your mother and I put bird food out today and saw some beauties. But they'll be cat food with all these strays running around. Here, take a look at what I found near your rope swing."

A few feet from the trap, beside her hideout bordering the woods, Alice saw a tiny bundle of bloody feathers and quickly looked away.

"Daddy, do you think animals go to Heaven?"

"I don't think anybody goes to Heaven."

Alice stood very still. If there wasn't any Heaven—and Alice was sure Grandmother planned on Pixie being there—how could there be a Hell? Who was she supposed to believe, her grandmother or her father?

"Then what happens to people who sin?" she asked.

"People who sin, whatever that means, will suffer the consequences on Earth. Or maybe they won't. Some people get away with murder."

"That's not fair."

"No. Life isn't," said her father, picking up the dead bird and laying it inside the trap. "I'll use the bird as bait."

Alice did not ask what he was going to do with the cats, and she did not go near the swing or the hideout. Instead, she went upstairs—slowly, because her head hurt—to do homework. When she finished, she turned to the back of her notebook and made a list of books—not counting the Black Stallion series or a bunch of Ben's Zane Gray adventures or repeats like *The Wind in the Willows* and *The Hobbit*—that she had read since the beginning of school: *The Call of the Wild, Treasure Island, The Three Musketeers, The Last Days of Pompeii, To Have and to Hold, The Virginian, Cyrano de Bergerac, Jean Christophe, A Tale of Two Cities, The Swiss Family Robinson,* and *Robinson Crusoe.* Most of them were long books, long enough to get lost in. She was just starting *The Count of Monte Cristo,* which had 1,365 pages. If her parents didn't catch her, she read with a flashlight under the blankets until two or three in the morning. The next day her eyes fuzzed and her head ached, but it was worth it. She usually made it through the week and slept late Saturday mornings.

Fridays were hard, though. By Friday, she was really tired. She should not have read late last night, because this Friday was special. The rich patient who lived in the mansion had invited her father to take the whole family out for a dinner "on the house"—which meant they didn't have to pay for it—in the hotel she owned on Lookout Mountain.

Alice imagined that the hotel was haunted by vampires, with a special suite for Dracula. She would not have spent a night alone there for a billion dollars, but dinner with the family would be thrilling. They had already decided to order steak, which Alice's mother bought only for birthdays. The fairy-tale lights of the Lookout Mountain hotel twinkled in Alice's mind, but they were clouded by her throbbing headache. The pain stayed with her standing up or lying down. Best not to move at all.

"Alice, it's time to get ready," called her mother.

Alice got up slowly and took her silky green dress off the hanger, pulled it over her head, and brushed her hair. Every move seemed to twist her eyeballs. The twinkling lights were turning into dancing black dots. When she went downstairs, everyone was waiting. Her mother wore her navy blue suit with the elegant short cape attached, her white blouse clasped with her cameo pin. Ben had no sports jacket, so he wore his school uniform, brass crossarms polished to a spit shine. Even her father, who never dressed up for anything, had put on a tie.

"All ready?" asked Alice's mother.

"Just a minute," Alice said, and raced to the small downstairs bathroom just in time to throw up. A few minutes later, her mother knocked on the door.

"Alice, are you all right?"

"I just have a headache."

Alice's mother eased into the room and felt her forehead. "Why didn't you tell me?"

Alice began to cry into the navy blue suit. "I didn't want to stay home."

"But honey, you can't go, you'd only be sick. We'd better let your father look you over."

"No, he'll get mad—he'll think I read late last night."

"Did you?"

Alice looked away.

"Well," said her mother, "you and I will just take it easy at home tonight. It will be okay. We'll make it cozy."

"But I don't want you to stay home, either."

"Alice, there are a lot of things more important than going out to dinner. Let me just send Ben on with your father now. I'll be right back."

Alice's mother returned after a few minutes, helped her up the stairs, eased the silky green dress off, and wrapped her in a soft bathrobe. Then she took off her blue suit, along with the white blouse and cameo pin, and put on her own robe. She brought aspirin and cool washcloths to fold over Alice's eyes. She rubbed Alice's forehead, pressed her temples where the pain was worst, and after a while began to read aloud from "East of the Sun and West of the Moon" in the old book of fairy tales. Alice let the words struggle and lift her over the sea and finally set her ashore. Slowly, slowly, relief set in, an easement of the terrible hammering in her head. Alice fell asleep cradled in her mother's voice.

The next morning, pain free, she wandered down the hall past Ben's room and stuck her head in his doorway. "Hey, Ben, did you and Daddy have a good time?"

"It was fun. You're supposed to knock on my door before you come in."

"I'm sorry, it was partway open. What did you eat?"

"Steak."

"I know that, but what else? Was it good?"

"Yeah, it was good."

"What did the restaurant look like?"

"It was fancy. You know, white tablecloths, lots of silverware, and waiters, and mirrors on the wall in gold frames, all that kind of stuff."

"It sounds like a palace."

"No, Dumbo, it was just a ritzy hotel."

That night they had corn on the cob, sliced tomatoes, and liver, which was cheap and nourishing. Alice ate a lot of corn and tomatoes.

"Don't Ben and Alice have spring vacation pretty soon?" asked Alice's father.

"Easter week," said Alice's mother.

"Could you take me horseback riding?" asked Alice. "You promised."

"We could do that. I was also thinking we could go camping. There's some land for sale on Brushy Creek Mountain, about an hour's drive from here."

Alice's mother looked down at her liver. "Ned, we've got to save our money. Ben's tuition is going up next year."

"So is the cost of land, Lydia. If we don't get it now, we won't get it at all. This would be a great investment—one hundred sixty acres of woods and fields with an old log cabin and barn and apple orchard, even a stream. There's some virgin timber that was there before any white settlers came through. The Cherokee hunted in those woods. You just don't find land like that in the mountains anymore. The paper companies are buying it all up for lumber."

"Well, I suppose it wouldn't hurt to look at it."

"If we buy it, we could probably rent out a couple of the fields and get our money back. We could also go out there every Sunday and plant a garden."

Alice and her mother looked at each other. Alice could see the empty spaces on her Church Chart stretching all the way to the end of the year. Miss Pilsen might not say anything, but the kids would. Miss Pilsen would just look at her the way Alice's grandmother used to look at her.

"Well, sometimes I would like to stay here and go to church," said Alice hesitantly.

"Look, we don't even know if we're going to buy this land or not." Alice's father got up impatiently and stalked off to listen to the news. Alice washed the dishes and Ben dried them, snapping his towel at her backside whenever he got ahead of her.

"Stop it, Ben."

"Well, speed it up. I don't have anything to dry."

"Here, dry your face, then." Alice flicked both her soapy hands at him, and Ben scooped a glassful back at her. Soon there was more soapy water on the floor than in the sink.

"Stop it, you two, and clean up that mess," said Alice's mother. But she smiled as she put away the leftover liver. Sunny watched her with drooling devotion. Sunny liked liver quite a lot better than Alice did.

That night Alice went up to her room with a clear head. She watched the lights go on across the valley far below her room. Suddenly the dark girl floated into her mind—a Cherokee girl who paddled her canoe upsteam one morning to gather watercress and returned to find her village in flames. From her canoe, hidden among the bushes arching the bank, she could see white army troops charging back and forth through the camp. Then they wheeled their horses around and thundered toward the stream. Quietly, she slipped the canoe around a bend, keeping to the shadowed bank. The shouts of the men and the screams from her village faded behind her. She was all alone.

Alice reached for her notebook and began to write.

The Mountain

Spring vacation dawned with a warm wind and a promise to go riding that day. Alice and her father started right after breakfast. Forgetting the map, he took a wrong turn and drove for an hour before they found the stable, but he was in a good mood. They opened their windows and sang "Oh, What a Beautiful Morning" as loud as they could, all the verses and the chorus, over and over.

The stable was old, and the groom was even older. He saddled a tall black gelding for Alice and a dancing bay mare for her father. Once Alice got up on the horse, she remembered why she had wanted to ride Lucky Jim, and also why she had been afraid to. On the trail, she was aware of being very far from the ground—too far from the ground and too close to the trees. As they started through the woods, Alice seemed to be getting closer and closer to the tree trunks. After a while, the horse began rubbing up against large oaks, mashing Alice's leg in the process.

"Don't let him get away with that. He'll rub you right off if he can," her father called from his bay mare, and he came by to give the gelding a whack on the rump. The gelding surged forward, caught Alice off balance, and thundered straight toward a steep, eroded embankment formed by an old mudslide. He wheeled to a stop just as he reached it. Alice collected her wits and her reins and turned the horse around.

"That's it," said her father. "You have to show him who's boss."

Alice's horse seemed to settle down then, and they rode along easily for several miles. She imagined herself traveling on the horses that carried the lass to the old women and the East Wind. Riding was not as hard as she had thought it would be, once the horse decided to cooperate. The path was soft with winter-worn leaves, and the branches overhead were beginning to send out bright green shoots. Across the path ahead ran a gentle stream of water. The gelding was behaving well now. When he dropped his head for a drink, Alice loosened the reins as she had seen movie-star cowboys do, leaning back in the saddle and picturing a sunset blazing the Western sky. The horse leaned, too. She doled out more rein. He must be thirsty after that run, thought Alice, as he buried his head, then his neck, in the water. Finally, he lay down entirely and rolled over. Alice was thrown free into the stream except for one leg, which he pinned for a split second before heaving up and setting off at a gallop for the stable. Alice's father checked her with a practiced eye and took off after the gelding. By the time she had crawled dripping up the bank and caught her breath, he reappeared leading the gelding behind him.

"I'm not getting back on," said Alice.

"You have to. If you don't, you'll be scared of horses for the rest of your life."

"That is a mean horse."

"He'll do what you want if you make him. This is something you shouldn't run away from."

It's the horse that ran away, not me, thought Alice, but she hauled her wet body back into the saddle. As her father predicted, the horse behaved all the rest of the way, except for a mad dash as they approached the stable.

Alice had never so appreciated climbing into a car. She rubbed her bruised leg and thanked her lucky stars that she owned a dog instead of a horse.

"Now that you've gone riding," said Alice's father on the way home, "we're going to spend the rest of the week camping. I've arranged to take some time off, and—amazing grace—your mother has no symphony rehearsals. We're going to explore that land up on Brushy Creek Mountain and then keep going till we have to come back."

Alice felt her father's restlessness fill the car like a leopard pacing its cage.

❖ ❖ ❖

The dirt road to Brushy Creek Mountain was so deeply rutted and washed out that they had to park the car and hike in. Rhododendron, holly, and hardwoods crowded the pathways through the property, and miles of old split-rail fence—made from chestnut trees, her father said—separated the fields from forest. The cabin itself was built of logs bigger than they'd ever seen. Inside, there was an old iron stove for heating and cooking, a broken table, an iron bed with a stained mattress, and rattlesnake skins stretched across the walls—some as long as Alice was tall.

The outhouse that served as a bathroom behind the cabin had lost half its roof. Beside the weathered barn, some long-ago settler had planted an apple orchard. The trees were gnarled and twisted into strange shapes. Several miles deeper into the woods, they came upon a chimney of blackened stones, standing alone in an overgrown clearing.

"The owner told me about this," said Alice's father. "There used to be another cabin here, beside that clear spring. The man who lived here had nine children. When his wife died, the oldest girl ended up taking care of all her brothers and sisters. One day she cleared them all out of the house and set it on fire. When her father came back from hunting, the whole place was burned to the ground and smoking. The kids were sitting there, waiting for him to take them away from Brushy Creek Mountain."

"Did he?" asked Alice

"I don't know. That's all of the story I heard, that the girl just went crazy from loneliness."

"It's beautiful country, but it is wild," said Alice's mother, looking up at the trees that towered over the old chimney.

"Yes, it is wild," said Alice's father, "and it's beautiful."

Alice knew at that moment that her father was going to buy the land no matter what her mother said.

They camped in the cabin that night, and Alice lay awake for a long time on her air mattress with Sunny nestled beside her. Through a broken window, moonlight reflected off the snakeskins lining the wall, and through her mind floated an old poem she had learned from a home-school book. There was a song to it. . . .

> Bed is too small for my tiredness.
> Give me a hill soft with trees.
> Tuck a cloud up under my head.
> Lord, blow the moon out please.

Through the window she could see the the white-eyed moon itself, and the dark outline of the mountain rising behind the barn. Somewhere out there in times past the settler's lonely daughter had watched the moon and planned to burn down her house. Somewhere out there, south of the sun and moon, the dark girl wandered without any house at all. Alice stroked Sunny's soft ears and stared at the mountain, repeating to herself like a prayer, "I will lift up mine eyes unto the hills, from whence cometh my help."

The next day, they drove toward the Great Smoky Mountain National Park, past forests draped with hemlock branches, meadows bristling with thistle, and streams that raced around rocks and fell suddenly into frothy waterfalls. Alice's father took Ben rock climbing down the face of a sheer granite drop, feeling his way from one ledge to the next.

"They should at least have ropes," raged Alice's mother. She would not let Alice go along, but Sunny lunged after them.

"I'll just carry him," said her father, and he bundled Sunny up in his old wool shirt and tied him to his back like a knapsack. Alice watched from the rim while they descended the cliff. When she closed her eyes, Alice could imagine them falling to the rocks below. When she opened her eyes, she could see how far they still had to go. But her father seemed to lead a charmed life. By the time Alice and her mother had wound their way down into the canyon on the service trail, her father and Ben had already started to set up camp, and Sunny ran cheerfully to greet them. That night it rained. When Alice dug a toilet hole with the folding shovel, water dripped down her back. Despite the drainage trench they had made around the tent, water formed little puddles in the floor, and wherever their bodies touched the sides of the canvas, wet spots spread. Alice longed for her snug bird's-nest bedroom, with rain painting city-light colors on the wet streets below.

As she folded their soggy blankets next morning, Alice's mother seemed anxious to get home, too. "We'd better start back today, Ned," she said. "We've got some hard driving ahead and only one more night."

They drove nonstop all morning, had a picnic lunch in a roadside park, and pressed ahead. Alice's father switched on the car radio for the afternoon news, in which everyone everywhere seemed to be fighting over everything. Alice did not want to hear about it.

"Locally," said the announcer, "there have been further reports of campers claiming to have sighted a mountain lion. Some say it's a fact, some say it's a hoax. We'll keep you posted." Alice's father swerved suddenly into a side road.

"What are you doing, Ned?" asked Alice's mother.

"Looking for a campsite."

"Keep going," Alice pleaded. "Don't stop here. It's not even dark yet."

"We'll get an early start on pitching the tent tonight," he said. "There'll be more light to see by."

All through the ritual of unpacking the food, driving tent pegs into the ground, and blowing up air mattresses, Alice kept glancing back over her shoulder at the thick woods surrounding them, perfect camouflage for mountain lions. When Ben foraged for wood, she prayed for his safe return. As the dark thickened, she looked for yellow eyes outside the circle of firelight.

After they all lay down in the tent with Sunny curled in the center, Alice tossed and turned, bumping into someone else with every move. She could not see the moon or the mountains, the dark girl was hiding, the air mattress was not blown up enough, the stones were sharp, Ben was breathing too loud, and Alice was barely breathing at all because she was holding her breath to listen for strange movements outside. She tried listening on her back, on her stomach, on her left side, and on her right side. At last her mother asked what was wrong, and Alice whispered her fear of the mountain lion, perhaps creeping up on them at this very moment.

Her father laughed softly from his place across the tent flap. "Maybe we should leave your noble dog outside to guard us."

"No! Sunny's staying inside tonight."

"Well, don't worry," he said, "to get you, this alleged mountain lion will have to get me first."

Alice spent the night listening, listening to an owl warning of intruders, listening to snapping twigs and rustling bushes. Crouched in her mind's eye was a tawny muscular body, hungry, waiting till everything was quiet, tensing toward her father . . . first.

The Church

"Do we have to go every week?" asked Alice.

"If we want to spend time with your father, we do."

The land on Brushy Creek Mountain was blooming with the warmth of spring. Wildflowers opened, leaves unfolded, and ferns uncurled. The twisted apple trees rained white blossoms. Animals came out of hibernation and rustled through the bushes. Alice's father spent every Saturday night and Sunday roaming the woods. He planted vegetables and began damming up the creek to make a pond. Ben helped him fix the outhouse, and they boarded over the holes in the cabin floor because rattlesnakes nested in the foundation underneath. Alice's father cut back the weeds with a swing blade and warned them to watch their step. Alice did her homework on the cabin porch and was careful where she walked.

On Sunday nights, they arrived back home, washed off the weekend's grime, and reorganized. On Mondays, Alice watched her section of the Church Chart stretch out in a blank white row. No one said anything. They didn't have to. Because of Alice, the class's church attendance record was never unanimous. All week, her eyes would stray to the chart even though she did not want to see it. She yearned to be in the gold-star line with everyone else. She craved gold stars. Then one Friday afternoon, Alice's end-of-the-week headache gave her an idea. After lunch on Saturday, she put her head down on the table. Her mother passed by on her way to and from the kitchen.

"What's wrong, Alice, don't you feel well?"

"My head hurts."

"Why don't you lie down and take a nap? We won't be leaving for Brushy Creek until your father finishes at the office this afternoon."

At 5:30, Alice heard her mother come up the stairs. Quickly she stuck her book under the pillow and began to think herself into a headache.

"Alice, you look terrible."

"I feel terrible."

"Maybe we shouldn't go out to Brushy Creek this time. You've got a headache. Ben has some tests next week, and I need to practice a new piece for the symphony. I'll talk to your father. He might be willing to stay home for a change."

Alice scrunched down in the bed and tried not to smile. On Monday morning, she would march to the front of the class beside Mary Jane McCall and stick a gold star on the chart. She could already taste the white gummy side of the star that she'd lick to make it sticky. Then Alice heard the back door slam downstairs and the car start. Her mother came back upstairs with a tight mouth.

"Did Daddy go?"

"He did."

Alice looked at her mother's angry face and began to feel the imaginary headache turn real. "I'm sorry."

"It's not your fault. You can't help being sick. And I suppose your father can't help being restless." Alice's mother sighed. "Do you want me to bring you some soup?"

"My stomach hurts, too. I'll just read for a while."

"Well, don't strain your eyes. It will just make the headache worse. I wish we knew more about what causes these headaches."

As soon as Alice's mother left the room, Alice buried herself in *Jean Christophe*. She was reading it for the second time. She could hear her mother tuning the harp downstairs. She could hear the buzzing of Ben's power drill. Sunny must have gone with her father or he would be curled up on her bed. Alice felt an uneasy twinge, but her contentment ruled. She wiggled her toes under the clean sheet. Before her stretched the free space of a snug evening, a safe bed, a warm bath in the morning, her silky green dress, the sunlit stained-glass windows of church, a Sunday dinner with no flies or mosquitoes hovering over it, a peaceful afternoon of reading, and on Monday morning, a gold star just like everyone else's.

Alice read late and slept late. After a quick breakfast, she barely had time to take a shower and get ready. Still, both the breakfast and the shower were hot, which was an improvement over the Brushy Creek cabin. The congregation was already singing the first hymn when they walked into church. Alice and her mother found the right page and joined the last chorus of "Joyful, Joyful, We

Adore Thee." Then everyone sat down with a rustle.

"That dress is getting too tight for you," whispered Alice's mother. "I need to make you a new one."

"Or buy one," whispered Alice. "We could go shopping."

Alice's mother smiled and took her hand. Alice closed her eyes and felt the minister's prayer float over the restful rows of bowed heads around her. She liked his accent. He was Scottish, which reminded Alice that she wanted to read *Lorna Doone* again when she finished *Jean Christophe*. After the prayer came a soprano's solo, "Listen to the Lambs, Calling," which sent shivers down Alice's spine. Then the minister rose again. His silver hair glowed like a star above the velvet stripes on his black robe.

"I want to speak today," he said in his soft burr, "about the secrets we keep from others, the secrets we keep from ourselves, and the secrets we keep from God."

Alice stared into the stained-glass windows. Their blue seemed deep enough to drown in, their reds fiery enough to burn. She listened to the rise and fall of the minister's voice. He did not shout like the preacher in Alabama, but held up an idea and looked at it from all sides, as if he were shaking a glass globe and watching snow fall around the figure inside.

The figure inside was Alice, trapped in her tight dress and the lie she had told.

The sermon was blessedly short, and Alice recovered from her guilt with the smell of chicken casserole filling the house when they returned from church. Ben had even set the table as penance for not going with them. The three of them had half finished their meal when the phone rang.

"I'll get it," said Alice. She scraped her chair back and ran into the living room.

"Dr. Ryder's's residence," she said into the mouthpiece.

"This is Dr. Talbot at the Good Samaritan Hospital in Libertyville."

"May I take a message? My father's not in right now."

"Your father's here in the emergency room. I need to talk with your mother."

Alice called her mother to the phone and went back to the table.

"Daddy's taking care of some kind of emergency in Libertyville," she said. "I guess he'll be late coming home."

"He's always late coming home," said Ben.

Alice's mother came back to the table, sat down, and stared at her plate.

"What's wrong?" asked Ben.

"Your father is unconscious, and they needed permission to do some surgery." Alice's mother put her hands over her face, then took them away again. "He was struck by a rattlesnake near an artery on his hand, and he must have passed out before he could do anything. He's lucky to be alive. The farmer who's renting the fields found him. Somebody got an ambulance halfway down that road and they packed ice around him to slow down the poison."

Ben put his forkful of food down and stared at Alice's mother. A red flush crept over his face. "It's his own fault," said Ben in a choked voice.

"Ben!"

"It's true. He bought that land knowing it was dangerous. You've seen the way he handles snakes. He probably tried to snap it by the tail, and it got him first."

"He knows what he's doing, Ben. He's been handling snakes since he was a boy in India."

"Well, if he wants to die, that's his business, but he shouldn't get his family killed in the process."

"Don't you dare talk about your father like that!"

Ben's chair fell backward as he stormed from the table and up the stairs. His door slammed, and there was silence. Alice saw tears slip between the thin fingers that covered her mother's face again.

"We should have been with him," whispered Alice. She got up to straighten Ben's chair. "Sunny! Where's Sunny? Sunny was with him."

"I don't know, Alice. The doctor didn't say. I have to drive up there now. You can come with me or stay here with Ben. We may not be back in time for school tomorrow."

"I'll go with you," said Alice in a small voice. She ran into her room, threw off her dress, and pulled on her old hiking jeans. Besides being too tight, the silky green dress reminded her of secrets from others, secrets from herself, and secrets from God.

The Hospital

Most of the way they rode in silence. Alice's mother gripped the steering wheel and stared at the road while Alice looked out her side window as the afternoon shadows reached toward the car. Her mind circled around her father . . . but surely her father could not die. Her heart circled around her dog. She knew her dog could die. He might be dead already, depending on what had happened. Fear like black clouds shaped scenes of Sunny snakebitten, Sunny hit by a car as he tried to follow her father to the hospital, Sunny cornered by a mountain lion in the deserted darkness of Brushy Creek Mountain. Alice shivered and tasted her own tears. She should be brave, she must be brave for her mother. *Nobody's too big to be scared. You just let your daddy have his snakes and pay him no mind.* But if her father died, he would be gone forever. She wished she had told him good-bye before he'd left. She wished she had told Leroy good-bye before he left.

When they got to the hospital, the doctor met them and asked Alice to stay at the nurses' station while he took

Alice's mother to the intensive care unit. Alice dared not ask about Sunny. She sat down in the clean, bright hall on a clean, bright chair and waited, with knuckles of pain tapping faintly at the back of her head. The nurses were kind. They asked Alice how old she was and where she went to school and whether she had any brothers and sisters. They told her that her father was strong and getting the best care in the world—there was nothing like a small-town hospital—and not to worry. They had not heard anything about her dog.

Alice's mother appeared several times looking pale and tired. Her hair curled wildly around her head, and under her gray eyes sagged half circles the color of a bruise. "He's doing as well as can be expected," she said to Alice. Later she came again and said he seemed to be out of immediate danger. "They're not sure about saving his hand."

"Did you ask about Sunny?"

"Ned's not really conscious yet, Alice. He just mutters sometimes, but I can't tell what he's saying. The doctor doesn't seem to know much about what happened, except medically, and the ambulance drivers are out on another call. We'll just have to wait."

"We should have been with him," Alice repeated what she had said to herself a million times. "You could have helped Daddy, and I could have held on to Sunny. You know how to cut a cross on snakebite and suck out the poison, and I—"

"Alice, don't. It's not your fault or my fault or your father's fault, even though he may have tempted fate. It was an accident."

Alice felt the weight of her lie twice over. Her mother did not even suspect her of faking a headache to stay home. If only she could confess so her mother would know whose fault it really was and forgive her, but the words stayed knotted in her stomach. The worst thing about this lie was that she might never be caught.

"It's getting late, Alice. Do you want any supper? There's a cafeteria somewhere downstairs."

Alice shook her head, and her mother hurried away again. As Alice wandered down the hallway to find a bathroom, she was startled to look out the window and see nighttime beyond the fluorescent light encircling her. She could not bear to think about Sunny out there in the dark, with snakes and mountain lions circling around him, and she could not bear to stop thinking about him. Her father seemed safe, at least, and getting better. She went back to the chair and waited.

Some time later—she didn't know how long because she must have fallen asleep—a skinny old man walked along the polished linoleum floor and stopped in front of her.

"Are you kin to the doctor that got snakebit up on Brushy Creek?"

She nodded up at him.

"Down in my truck I got somebody awful anxious to make contact with the family. Short tail, long ears, kind of reddish fur?"

At first Alice did not understand him. She felt packed in cottonish fog. Then the words clicked into place. "Sunny!" she cried.

"Reckon that's who it is. I rent a field from your daddy, and that dog's a regular visitor, just about every time your daddy shows up."

The old man turned to the nurse. "Flora, you mind if I take this girl down to see her dog? He's full of burs, but I reckon she'll be glad to see him."

"Go ahead, George. I'll tell her mother. They could use a little cheering up about now."

"What happened to Sunny? What happened to my father?"

"I don't rightly know about your father, because by the time I got there he was pretty far gone and the dog wasn't talking, but I loaded them both into my truck and headed for the highway. Stopped at the nearest neighbor's phone and called the ambulance—my truck's pretty slow. It's good enough to haul corn, but you wouldn't want to trust it going fast down the mountain. So here comes that ambulance with the siren yammering and the lights swirling and soon as I open the truck door so they can get your daddy, the dog shoots out like a cannonball and hightails it to who knows where. We weren't so concerned about the dog just then. But after they packed up your daddy, I started thinking maybe I'd better track him down—the dog, that is—so I did, but it took a while. Quite a while. That dog can move."

The elevator had taken them downstairs and the revolving door had chased them onto the front sidewalk before the old man took a breath and stuck out his hand. "My name's George Tate. Glad to meet you. That's my truck over there—I finally got it down the mountain—and that black nose stuck out the window is likely picking up your scent this very minute."

Alice ran toward the truck with the old man hobbling after her. She thrust her hands through the top of the window he had left open for air and pressed her face against the glass. Sunny whined and yelped inside.

"Here, here, hold on a minute, you young ones are so all-fired hasty. Just pull on the handle, the door's not locked, nobody in their right mind would steal this truck. I wish they would so I could get the insurance. Your daddy might get some insurance, this being an accident and all, though I have to say that nobody in their right mind would hang around that cabin very long, there's enough rattlers there to scare off a nitwit, with all due respect. Now stop slobbering on each other, you're going to mess up my best truck. This here's my best truck. It's also my only truck, so I'm lucky it's the best one."

Alice was squeezing Sunny tight in her arms, Sunny was frantically licking her face, and George Tate was climbing into his truck.

"Wait!" said Alice. "Are you leaving?"

"Well, I gotta get on home. You tell your mama that I hope your daddy gets well soon, and take this piece of rope and put it around that dog's neck so he doesn't make another break for it if one of those ambulances sets up a howl. They're not supposed to let dogs into the hospital, but Flora's my niece and you just tell her that I took off and left you with nowhere to put the dog and she'll chew me out after church next Sunday but she'll let your dog stay with you while you wait, which seems like a good idea. What's your name, anyway?"

"Alice."

"Hello, Alice. You're the first person I ever met named Alice, except Alice in Wonderland, who I never met, anyway, and that's a fact. Well, you get on in there, I'll watch you to the door, and don't go playing around that cabin, you or your dog, either, or your daddy for that matter, though maybe he's learned his lesson."

The truck started with a roar that rocked Alice backward and sent Sunny struggling in her arms and prickling her with the burs he'd collected in his great escape. From a cloud of blue exhaust, she hurried toward the door, waved at George Tate, and watched him inch the truck out of the parking lot.

"Thank you," she called, too late. He could never have heard her over the din. But she was smiling for the first time in hours. People could disappear, but sometimes, just as unexpectedly, people could appear, for which Alice was deeply grateful. And Sunny, too. She put him down, tied the rope around his neck, just in case he heard a siren, and gathered him back in her arms, marching up the stairs—no point in risking the elevator—to confront Flora with Uncle George's instructions. It was going to be a long night, but Alice could spend it picking out burs.

The Story

Alice's father slowly recovered, but his hand—even after two operations and skin grafting—was scarred and strangely misshapen. His hand reminded her of the old apple trees twisted into strange shapes by the wind on Brushy Creek Mountain. The sight of her father's hand made Alice look away. At mealtimes, she looked down at her plate while he ate.

"We're going to have to hire a part-time nurse until this hand heals," he said one night at dinner. "I can't keep up at the office."

He could not keep up because of the pain, Alice knew, and she knew that he would never say that. "I could help," said Alice, "after school and on Saturdays."

"You're not a nurse, Alice," said her mother.

"Well, it's not a bad idea, though," said her father. "She could free the nurse and receptionist to help me more. Alice could answer the phone, pull charts and file them—we're way behind on filing—and she could get supplies when we need them and clean up the waiting room, or just talk to the patients when they get impatient."

The last job turned out to be the hardest. Her father's waiting room was always jammed because he still treated patients on his old first-come, first-served basis. But they had to be more patient than ever because he was not always there to serve. Sometimes he was away on house calls or hospital calls. Sometimes he simply walked in an hour or two late.

"He had an emergency," Alice explained, but she wondered if some of the emergencies were of his own making, if getting lost on a house call meant finding a woodsy place to stop and hike on a workday. And despite his narrow escape on Brushy Creek Mountain, he returned there every weekend, with or without the family.

"I just made a mistake," he told Alice. "I picked up what I thought was a harmless black snake and it turned out to be a young rattler still dark from shedding its skin." Alice's father squeezed the rubber ball with which he constantly exercised his lame hand. "It was not my lucky day. But remember, Alice, when the going gets tough, the tough get going." Alice looked away from his twisted thumb and fingers working rhythmically to regain their strength and flexibility.

At the end of the month, Alice helped send out bills. Then she opened the checks that people sent back to pay the bills. There were more bills than checks. A lot of people owed her father money, which he did not seem to notice. Alice's mother noticed.

"You've been wonderful to help out in the office, Alice," she said one evening as Alice struggled with her math homework at the kitchen table. "I don't know what your father would have done without you. He really can't afford to hire someone else right now, but this is taking all of your free time."

"That's all right. I can work more hours in the summer."

"Some of the summer. We'll be going back to Alabama to visit with your grandparents and take a little vacation."

"Do we have to?"

"I thought you'd want to. Wouldn't it be nice to see your Grandmother again?"

"I don't know." Alice leaned over and stroked Sunny, who always helped out with difficult assignments by lying across her feet. "Sometimes Grandmother was nice and sometimes she wasn't."

"She's human, honey. People are always more complicated than we think."

"Not all of them."

"Such as who?"

"Oh, I don't know. Jimmy Breckinridge. He's never nice."

"Jimmy Breckinridge has his own story. We just don't know what it is."

"So that makes it okay for him to be mean?"

"I didn't say people were always justified. I said they were always complicated. It helps to try to understand why."

"What about Daddy? Why is he so complicated?"

"Partly because his parents were so busy doing missionary work that they sent him off to a boarding school that treated him badly."

"He loved that school."

"They beat him there, Alice, and he was miserable. He

just doesn't talk about that part of it. I think that's why he tried to toughen himself up with dangerous things like handling snakes, to handle those feelings. That's probably why he's always trying to toughen you and Ben up."

"Why did his parents send him away?"

"That's complicated, too. They believed they were doing God's will."

"If it's all so complicated, how can you tell whether you're doing right or wrong?"

"Look in your heart. Look in your mind. Look around you. And still, Alice, sometimes you have to make choices where no way seems right. Or you make wrong choices even if you know what's right."

"Then what do you do?"

"Keep trying."

✣ ✣ ✣

On the last day of school, Mrs. Hopkins asked everyone to clean out their desks and stack the textbooks on a table.

"Good riddance!" said Jimmy Breckinridge.

"You know, Jimmy," said Mrs. Hopkins, "you might want to try getting used to schoolwork. You've got seven more years left even if you don't go to college."

"Well, I've got the whole summer free now and I don't have to read a book for three months."

Alice stared at Jimmy Breckinridge. Freedom *was* reading a book.

"My parents are sending me to camp," said Mary Jane McCall.

"A camp for morons," said Jimmy Breckinridge.

"A camp just for girls, thank goodness."

"Good riddance!" shouted Jimmy Breckinridge.

Alice smiled. It was a relief to see Jimmy Breckinridge picking on someone else, someone who didn't care. Sometime during the spring—Alice wasn't sure exactly when because she was more worried about her father than about having friends—the game of taunting Alice had petered off to silence. Alice was alone on an island surrounded by silence. She was not exactly happy there, but at least no one crossed over to harass her.

Miss Pilsen handed out gift-wrapped Bibles to the students who had perfect records of church attendance. Alice looked away from the rows of gold stars shining across the Church Chart. In the island of white spaces beside her name was a gold star that almost cost her father's life—he who had almost cost others their lives, and saved lives as well. What kind of gold stars shone beside her father's name? She looked out the window, where the blue ridges seemed to stretch southward forever. *I will lift up mine eyes unto the hills, from whence cometh my help. My help cometh from the Lord, which made heaven and earth. He will not suffer thy foot to be moved. He that keepeth thee will not slumber. Behold, he that keepeth Israel shall neither slumber nor sleep. The Lord is thy keeper. The Lord is thy shade upon thy right hand. The sun shall not smite thee by day nor the moon by night. The Lord shall preserve thee from all evil. He shall preserve thy soul. The Lord shall preserve thy going out and thy coming in from this time forth and even for evermore.*

"Boys and girls," said Miss Pilsen, "even if you didn't win a Bible, this is a record that most of you can be proud of. Next year, let's make it even better. Have a wonderful summer. And don't forget to go to church."

Nobody seemed to be listening to Miss Pilsen. She backed out of the room smiling as students cleaned out the fish tank, the hamster cage, and the turtle dish.

"And don't forget to return your library books," said Mrs. Hopkins. She walked over to the Church Chart, rolled it up, and snapped a rubber band around it. Alice felt a huge weight lifted from her shoulders. On her way out of the room with a pile of library books, she stopped at Mrs. Hopkins's desk and laid down a folder.

"What's this, Alice?"

"I wrote that story. You know, about the picture?"

"Good for you!"

"It took me all year."

"Some stories take longer than others."

"And it's not even very long."

"Some stories are shorter than others. I'm just glad you worked on it, Alice, and that you're letting me read it. I'll send it back to you with a note after I've finished."

Alice thought about the story on her way home. The dark girl had escaped downstream from the troops, but her canoe was wrecked by rocks as she paddled through some rapids. She managed to grab the overhanging branch of a tree and pull herself onto a small island before the canoe sank. There she had made a shelter and lived off fish and summer berries till she could build a raft. It was a lonely life, but she survived.

"He got out alive, didn't he?"

"But he got hurt."

"Sometimes it hurts to get out alive. Live and learn."

Alice could see now that the story was not really finished, and there were parts that needed changing. Into her mind came the lass who set out with the bear in "East of the Sun and West of the Moon." That lass had been lonely, too, and survived. By the time Alice opened her own door, she had an idea of what might happen next. The dark girl was going to leave the island and find a bear cub whose mother had been killed by hunters. Then she could raise the bear cub and . . . what? Alice would find out. She had all summer to work on it.

Alice's mother smiled up at her from the harp without missing a beat. The metronome was going again, tock, tock, tock, tock, tock. Her mother's fingers shaped the scales like Leroy hitting nails, each note strong and sure, each note determined and even.

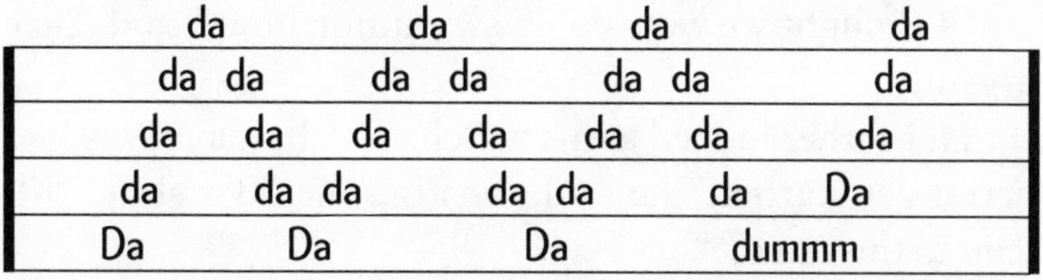

da da da da

da da da da da da da

da da da da da da da

da da da da da da Da

Da Da Da dummm

The sound of Ben's own hammering punctuated the beat—bang, bang, bang, bang. Who knows how far a hammer rings, who knows how far a sweet sound sings?

Her father came out of the kitchen carrying a bowl of milk. Sunny darted from behind him, suddenly torn between greeting Alice and following the bowl of milk. Sunny was quite devoted to milk, and the choice was hard. He gave a happy bark in her direction but stayed close to her father's feet, just in case the bowl was suddenly set down on the floor.

"You're home early, Daddy," said Alice.

"I declared a holiday and closed the office. We're going swimming in the lake."

Alice followed her father out into the yard, with Sunny tangling in between their legs.

"What's the bowl for?"

Alice watched her father approach the cat trap, untwist the lock, and open the door a crack. He's feeding the wild cats, she thought, with a small flutter of hope. Sunny leaped toward the cage, barking suddenly and then backing away with hackles raised. Her father slid the bowl toward a mangy cat huddled in the corner as far from human hands as possible.

"Those who are about to die deserve milk," he said softly.

Alice stood still. She had known in her secret heart that he wouldn't catch stray cats just to let them go again.

"I thought we were going swimming now," said Alice urgently.

Her father looked at his watch. "Well, maybe we had better get started," he said, twisting the door shut. "I'll tend to this later."

While her father rounded up Ben and her mother, Alice grabbed a bathing suit and towel. Then she ran back outside, latching the dog door behind her to keep Sunny in the house.

The trap was set into a dark thicket where cats would likely hide a den. The cat was huddled in the same corner, but the milk was gone. He was not a pretty cat. He watched her through slitted green eyes, his mottled black-and-orange fur—like fire cracking the alligator's back—pressed against the wire cage. She remembered pressing her hand against the wire screen of the sleeping porch in Alabama. *You just think what it would be like to live in a big white cage all the time, honey.*

Even without a cage you could be trapped, south of the sun and moon. She was reading herself free, she was writing herself free, she was surviving by stories, but the cat could not. She must let the cat go. Her father would be furious, but she'd survive that, too. Alice leaned over, unlatched the wire cage, and opened it. The cat crouched down, hissed at her once, and was gone. Nothing else moved except the sunlight that slanted past her like an open doorway. Alice stood up and walked through it. *Home free.*

AUTHOR'S NOTE

Most of the events in this book actually happened, with some change of detail, reshaping of sequence, and compression of time. By 1953 the Korean War had ended, but the war on segregation was just beginning. The Supreme Court's decision that segregated schools were unconstitutional *(Brown v. Board of Education),* to which Alice's teacher refers, came in May of 1954. The Montgomery bus boycott, which Alice's father mentions, started right after Rosa Parks was arrested on December 1, 1955, for refusing to give up her seat for a white person as the bus driver demanded.

In addition to the incidents described in this book, many others both worse and better happened to me while I was growing up in Alabama and east Tennessee during the 1940s and 1950s. One of the better experiences involved some time spent in a camp called The Highlander Folk School. It was run by friends of my mother's, the Shipherds, from Oberlin, and it was a liberal (considered radical, in those days) place where Rosa Parks and others as courageous as she went for discussion, support, and fellowship in their civil rights work. The first day I went swimming there was the first time in all my experience of Southern pools, ponds, creeks, rivers, lakes, and beaches that I had seen adult whites and blacks swimming together. Even as a preadolescent, I knew something momentous was happening. At this moment I can still feel what I felt then: that the world can be reborn. Despite the necessary labor pains, the South is a different world for today's children.

Other controversial Supreme Court rulings prohibited

prayer and Bible reading in the public school systems *(Engel v. Vitale, 1962; Abington School District v. Schempp, 1963)*. For children outside the mainstream religion, it was a relief. For those inside, it was a loss. One person's victory is another person's defeat. Individuals are always fighting private wars—with themselves, their families, their schools, and their society. What we don't realize is how often these private wars are entwined with public wars, and how important is each person's peace.